Chosen for Power

Women of Power Series

Kathleen Brooks

Prologue

Elle Simpson tugged at the old dress she was wearing. It had been her mother's. Just as her younger sisters wore her castoffs, Elle wore her mother's when there was no money for new clothes. Her cheeks were scrubbed clean and her golden-red hair was pulled into a tight braid that hung down her back as she stood tall in the hand-me-downs.

Her mother gently pushed Elle and her sisters forward while the woman in the black suit looked down at her with a forced smile. Bree and Allegra, Elle's younger sisters, tightened their grips on Elle's hands while Reid, her older brother, stood directly behind her with his hand on her shoulder. They looked up at the woman as a group and waited as her mother pleaded her case.

"Please understand, Mrs. Henson. My husband is gone most of the year fixing the railroads. He always sends his checks home, but sometimes they take a while to get here, depending on where he's working. I promise, I'll have the money."

"Mrs. Simpson," the lady said with a sigh, "I'm sorry, but I'm running a school, not a charity."

Elle felt her family stiffen collectively. They did not take handouts. They may be poor, but they were proud.

"I'm not asking for charity, Mrs. Henson," her mother

said, offended. "I have never missed paying a bill, and I won't miss this one. I'll have the tuition by the end of the month. Please, just let my kids enroll."

Mrs. Henson took in the hand-me-down clothes with scuffed shoes and shook her head. Elle felt her temper flare. Sure, they weren't rich like the other kids at the school their mother was determined to send them to, but that didn't mean they weren't good enough.

"Mother, I think the better question would be whether Mrs. Henson can convince us Winsor Academy is good enough. Since Temple Park is offering us full scholarships, I think we should go there. After all, we're the smartest kids in our school," Elle said with as casual a voice she could muster.

"Temple Park?" Mrs. Henson asked with surprise.

"That's right," Reid said before their mother could tell Mrs. Henson that Winsor's biggest rival had offered them no such thing. In reality, they'd laughed at their mother for even applying there for admission into the other elite private school. "They said something about helping them win the Academic Bowl." Reid shrugged with a bored look as he glanced around Mrs. Henson's impressive office.

"Well, I guess it wouldn't hurt to do some testing. School starts in two days so we need to move fast. I'll have you each meet with our counselors for an academic test, and then I'll let you know tomorrow. Just promise me that you won't agree to Temple until we can revise our offer." Mrs. Henson hurried through her desk pulling out papers and writing brief notes on them.

"I promise," Elle's mother said, hiding the relief in her voice.

Two days after they aced every test Mrs. Henson put in

front of them, Elle took a seat by herself in the cafeteria of Winsor Academy. Her brother and the rest of the freshmen ate later in the day. Her younger sisters had already had their lunch break, so there was no one for Elle to sit with. So far no one had spoken to her. They all just looked at her and whispered. Some laughed, others made snide comments about her to their friends loud enough for her to hear, but they never talked to her. It had taken the other kids three minutes to find out Elle's family lived in the poor section of town and they didn't have a nanny, a driver, or a butler. They weren't from Old Atlanta society and, therefore, were not one of them.

"Excuse me, is this seat taken?" The soft, flawless southern voice caused Elle to cringe as she anticipated being picked on once again.

Looking at the owner of the voice, Elle felt like throwing in the towel. The girl next to her was drop-dead gorgeous. She had long, wavy blond hair with ice-blue eyes shining brightly. She stood with a soft smile on her full pink lips as she looked down at Elle.

"No," Elle answered a little hesitantly as she moved her tray over some.

"Mallory! What are you doing talking to *her?* Our table is over here, remember?" a girl with a big bow around her ponytail asked with a look of horror on her face.

"She must have forgotten over the summer," teased another girl with a matching bow in her hair.

Elle watched as Mallory stiffened but put her tray down next to Elle's anyway. "Thanks, but not today. I'll see you at cheer practice." She sat down amid the outrage of her friends and smiled. "Hi. I'm Mallory Westin."

Elle may have only been at the elite school for half a day, but even she knew the name Westin. It was everywhere: Westin Library, Westin Field. And now Mallory Westin was sitting with her. "I'm Elle Simpson," she said, looking around to see if she was going to have chili or something else dumped on her. "I'm sorry, but why are you here?"

Mallory laughed a bit without a hint of offense at the question. "I've heard all about you. I wanted to get to know you better, especially since you've made it this far without crying. They've been pretty harsh, haven't they?" she asked, gesturing to the people in the cafeteria.

Oh yeah, they'd been harsh. They'd whispered horrible things, just loud enough for her to hear. They'd knocked her books from her hands, and she had been smashed in the face by a dodge ball in gym class. "And you're not one of them?" Elle asked with a hint of sarcasm. "No, you're not one of them; you're the queen bee and can order your minions as you please."

"That's right, I belong to the same clubs, have my last name plastered everywhere, and even have followers. But I never said I like it. I'm much more than just my parents' name," Mallory said.

Elle thought she saw a flash of steely resolve beneath her glossy smile. "Well then, have a seat. It's nice to meet you, Mallory."

Chapter One

The smell of sesame chicken made her mouth water. Elle Simpson thanked the guy behind the counter of her favorite take-out restaurant and took the bag of food. It would be another dinner alone after a long day at work. The thought of slipping off her heels and settling in for a night on the couch sounded perfect after the exhausting day.

Elle opened the brown bag and smiled when she saw the extra fortune cookies they threw in for her.

"Hey! Watch where you're going."

"Oh, sorry. I was . . ." Elle's eyes narrowed and then widened in shock. Chord McAlister, the son of a bitch who had dated her only to steal inside info against her family's business, stood in front of her with his arm around her old roommate and friend.

"Rebecca? What's going on?" Elle stuttered as she looked between the two. Her heart pounded as she felt a stab of betrayal deep within her.

"What does it look like? I'm on a date," her old friend snapped.

Elle looked back to Chord and took him in. She hadn't seen him in eight years. Not since his failed attempt to take over her company and subsequent downfall. He was still Chord, though: expensive suit, smooth smile, perfect hair.

And the smug look on his handsome face told her he hadn't changed at all during his exile.

"I didn't know you were back."

"You don't know a lot of things, babe."

Eww. Elle might have loved that endearment when they were dating, but now it gave her the shivers. "Becca, I don't understand. What are you doing with Chord?"

"Just because he wasn't good enough for the almighty Elle doesn't mean he isn't good enough for us mere mortals," Becca spat. Her beautiful brown hair was pulled up in a sleek ponytail that swayed with anger as she spoke.

Elle felt as if she had been punched in the stomach. Becca had been her sorority sister in college and then they'd been roommates after graduation. Becca had gone on to work at a television company while Elle went to get her master's in business. "But, you know what this man did to me. You were there. You saw it all. How could you be with him?"

"Playing the victim again, Elle? You're so good at that, aren't you? Can you never take responsibility? He told me how you made up the whole story about him."

"Becca, he tried to take over my company! He tried to destroy me and everything my family had worked for."

Chord smiled and Elle wanted nothing more than to slam her fist into his perfect face. She should have known something wasn't right when he had pushed her out of the bathroom so he could do his hair in the mornings.

"I told you she'd say that. After all the horrible things she told me about you. It's just jealousy. She saw you and I had chemistry so she got between us, just like she's trying to do now. If she can't be happy, then no one can," Becca said with a smirk. "Going home alone to eat dinner in your pajamas?"

The barb hit home. Elle felt the tears pushing on the back of her eyes, but she refused to let them fall. She pushed her shoulders back and raised her chin in defiance. "If you're happy, Becca, then so am I. Have a good evening."

Elle gave her old friend a weak smile and hurried to her car before she could no longer contain her tears.

"That son of a biscuit!" Mallory cursed in her own way as she took a bite of the sesame chicken and kept her eyes on the monitor in front of her.

"Thanks for the support. It was horrible. They made me feel like I was nothing, worse actually." Elle had called her best friend as soon as she got into the car. Mallory was on a job, but like a true friend, she told her to come straight over. "Mal, am I really as pathetic as they made me sound? I never thought of myself that way before."

Mallory reached out and squeezed her hand. "I've known you for what, twenty years? You're one of the strongest women I know, and you have never once allowed yourself to wallow like you're doing now. Chord McAlister is old news. You dumped his derriere seven years ago while destroying his reputation and the company he worked for. For crying out loud, he's been in exile for years. I wouldn't call that pathetic. I'd call that strong."

Elle felt a smile tug at her face. She shouldn't feel good about it, but she did. "I couldn't have done it without your help."

"Hey, what are friends for?" Mallory smiled. "Oh, there's my guy. He's been trespassing on this singer's property and breaking into her house leaving her little gifts. I'll be right back."

Mallory pressed a button, setting off the silent alarm,

and hopped out the back of the utility truck. She strode toward the nervous-looking man lurking in the shadows near the gate of a massive estate. Elle almost felt sorry for him as she watched on the monitor. Mallory's long blond hair fell in perfect waves over her shoulders and her heels accented her slim legs encased in black skinny jeans as she walked toward the man, now trying to find a way over the brick wall. Poor sucker. Mallory was the epitome of the saying "Don't judge a book by its cover."

Elle slipped off her heels and put her feet up on the table. She hated heels almost as much as she hated Chord. Reaching for some lo mein, Elle shook her head in pity as the man failed to notice Mallory's approach. Right before he wiggled his way over the top of the wall, Mal grabbed his feet and yanked him down. One perfect spiked heel rested on his chest as she talked down at him. Elle heard sirens in the distance and cleaned up the leftovers as she thought about what her best friend had said.

She wasn't pathetic or weak. She had never folded or complained about her life. No, she had worked hard since she was a child. She didn't begrudge her friend falling in love even though she'd never experienced it. And she certainly wasn't going to let a prick like Chord make her feel bad about herself. Chord was just trying to tear her down but she refused to let him. And she had the charity ball tomorrow where she intended to be very unlike the Elle most people knew. She was going to mingle, flirt, and maybe, just maybe, find someone to have dinner with.

Elle tapped her bunny-slippered foot as she signed the final paper to purchase a controlling share in a Swiss bank. She put her pen down and closed the folder. The documents needed to be scanned and sent to the bank before their teleconference early the next morning.

When she closed the folder, she caught sight of a picture on the corner of her desk. It had been taken eight years ago at the lake her family visited for one week every year. Her father had his arm around Elle and her mother. Her older brother and two younger sisters stood arm in arm beside them. It was the last family picture they had taken before her father had died unexpectedly from a massive heart attack.

"Miss Simpson?" Elle looked away from her family picture to the tired face of her secretary.

"Yes, Jessica?"

"It's nine o'clock and the last bus to my house leaves in thirty minutes. If you're done with the papers, I can email them and be on my way."

Elle looked at the clock and instantly felt like a grinch. She was keeping Jessica from her family at Christmas time. "I'm sorry to keep you so late. I can take care of the email. And I don't want you having to take the bus home so late at night. Please, take the limo. He'll pick you up downstairs." Elle turned in her chair and buzzed her driver, Finn, on the intercom.

"But you need to get to the Drake Charles Foundation Ball," Jessica protested.

"I don't need to be there until ten and Finn will be back by then. Have a merry Christmas." Elle stood up and walked around her desk. She hugged her secretary before handing her a card.

"What's this?"

"Your Christmas present. Say hi to Dan and the boys for me." Elle went over to the scanner in the corner of her downtown Atlanta office. She heard Jessica tear open the envelope and then gasp.

"But, you've already given us our bonuses," Jessica stammered.

"I know. This is your Christmas present. Now, if you hurry, you may be able to stop and get those bikes your boys asked Santa for." Elle turned from feeding the scanner and was enveloped in a tight hug.

"You're the best. Thank you." Jessica hugged her again and then hurried from the room only to return with an elaborate box. "The ball is a masquerade. I ordered this for you."

Elle tried not to roll her eyes. Drake Charles was eccentric, so a masquerade ball seemed to be a perfect extension of his personality. She wondered if he would even be there. Charles had built a fortune through smartphone technology, but he wasn't a front-page-of-*Forbes*-type guy. There were rumors he was a recluse—that he was deformed, or possibly on his deathbed. Nobody seemed to know much about him. All she knew was he gave millions of dollars every year to the same children's hospital Elle's family supported.

Elle opened the box and pulled out a beautiful gold mask with pale pink swirls. It was elegant in its simplicity. There were no feathers or elaborate designs—just simple swirls, a pink lining around the eyes, and a matching pink satin ribbon. "Thank you, Jessica. This will match my dress perfectly."

"Remember, you have the call with the Swiss bank at two in the morning, eight their time, so they can conclude the deal and file the paperwork before they close their offices at noon. Then you need to be at your mother's around eight. Good night, Miss Simpson. Merry

Christmas."

"Merry Christmas." Elle waited for Jessica to leave before she finished sending the email to the bank's board of directors and completed the necessary paperwork for the teleconference later that night.

Elle took a tired breath and stood up to stretch as she looked out over the lights of the city. Her mind was still on her family. This business deal would solidify their standing in the world marketplace. Her family had never been as wealthy as they were now, but they'd always been happy. Her father had been a railroad worker and had traveled most of the year to work on various projects. They felt fortunate that he had a job at all. The dangerous and back-breaking work had provided them with a better-than-average income. Her mother had used that increased income to send the kids to Winsor Academy, but they'd never moved from their small house. One night before he left on a four-month tour, her father had told them he had developed a five-year plan to change the fortune of the family. For those five years, the only extra money they had spent was on their schooling. Everything else was put into savings.

Her father seemed to have aged three times as fast from the hard work, but they had a large nest egg. The government had deregulated the railroad industry and small tracks of railroad had been put up for sale. Her father had purchased one of the sections, cleaned it up, and then charged the larger railroad companies for the rights to use it. When her father's new company started turning a profit, he'd bought more sections of railroad in addition to shares of energy companies, steel companies, and even financial services.

But then Elle's father had died when she was just twenty-five. Her mother was devastated and the company had began to flounder as Elle took charge. Her older brother by two years had been trying to "find himself," yet he had had no trouble finding his trust fund to enjoy in Europe. Bree, at twenty-three, had been fresh out of college and headed to get her master's while Allegra was only twenty-one and still in college. None of her siblings were ready to take on that kind of responsibility. Elle had earned an MBA and had been working at a low-level job in the company when she had suddenly advanced to president and CEO.

She had immediately proven herself by fighting off a takeover attempt—one that Chord helped plan and execute. Once she had gotten behind the big desk, she had decided that Simpson Operations could be bigger. She had changed the name to Simpson Global and had enlisted the help of her family—the only people willing to believe in her. Her youngest sister, Allegra, loved fashion and had begun purchasing several mid-sized fashion houses with a little help from the family's financial holdings. Soon Allegra had become the executive vice president of Simpson Fashion.

Her other sister, Bree, had shown interest in the construction side of the company and had taken over Simpson Steel. A year later, her brother, Reid, had approached her with an idea: hotel casinos. He'd been in Monaco for several years. Instead of losing his trust fund, he had actually doubled it. He had fallen in love with the casino business. Elle had agreed to lend him enough money to start up Simpson Hotels and Casinos, including the purchase of a small casino, which he had then turned into the number-two casino in all of Europe. Within five years, he had opened three more casinos across the globe that were all thriving.

The first thing Elle did as CEO was hire Mallory's security company. She was happy to be Mallory's first client. Simpson Global was now a multi-billion-dollar international conglomerate and her father's vision was complete.

Elle groaned as she looked down at the floppy ears of her slippers. She had forgotten to slip her heels back on when Jessica came in. Oh well, her secretary knew everything already. She had to be aware of the comical slippers hidden under Elle's desk.

She kicked off the bunny slippers and glided over the thick carpet to her private closet. She reached in and unzipped the garment bag to pull out the pale pink haute couture gown. She had fallen in love with it when her sister had sent her a picture, suggesting she wear it to the ball. It definitely was not "her," and that was why she loved it.

Elle's closet consisted of suits — tons and tons of fitted suits with blouses and matching heels. Then she had gowns. Boring gowns that made her feel sixty instead of thirty-three. Heaven forbid a CEO wear a slinky, sexy gown that showed some cleavage or flashed a little leg. CEOs were pillars of the business world and it was considered bad form to remind anyone you might be a woman with a sensual side. But, tonight this CEO was breaking the rules. Tonight Elle was leaving behind the boring suits and the silent rules of behavior. She was going to leap into the masquerade. She was going to do and say all the things she had longed to because no one would know who she was tonight.

Elle sat down and started the work of teasing and pinning her hair until she looked just like one of those models on a catwalk. Her hair had height, volume, and was pinned back from her mask. Her long golden tresses hung in sleek waves down her back. She wore only foundation on her face, but used the matching pink eye shadow to shade all around her green eyes. When her mask was on, the pink around her eyes blended and made the mask look as if it were a part of her.

Finally it was time to try on the dress. She slipped on the incredibly sexy gown that fastened at her neck with a jeweled necklace. Two lengths of beaded chiffon draped from the necklace, barely covering her full breasts before crisscrossing over her flat stomach and flowing to the floor as if made from long scarves. The full satin skirt, slit to the upper thigh, flashed just the right amount of skin whenever she walked. It was daring, naughty, and, most of all, exciting. It made her feel powerful and womanly at the same time.

Her phone rang and she slipped on her heels as she went to answer it. "Miss Simpson, I'm back and waiting out front," Finn said.

Elle grabbed her small clutch and stuffed her lip gloss and phone into it before riding the elevator down the forty-five floors. She had met Finn the night her father had had a heart attack. She had been running errands for the company while her father had spent the day with her mother. Finn had been the cab driver who had escorted a hysterical Elle to the hospital. He had shown her so much compassion that day and she'd never forgotten it. In the months following her father's death, she'd requested Finn from the cab company whenever she had needed a cab.

After Simpson Global took off, her mother had started lecturing her. "I don't like the idea of a young woman wandering around alone. You need to be more careful."

Elle had bought a couple of cars for the business and had told Finn she'd triple his salary if he came on as head driver for Simpson Global. Even though he was a couple of years younger than she was, he'd taken on a paternal and very protective role in her life. He'd looked out for her and her sisters and had been someone she could entrust with her secrets.

Finn was waiting for her when she pushed open the large glass door to the building. He stood by the limo in a white button-up shirt that contrasted with his dark skin and fit snuggly over his large, muscular shoulders. Finn had been a first baseman in the Atlanta Braves minor league farm system before a knee injury ended his career. After all these years, he still looked as if he played. When he saw her, Finn's brown eyes widened. "Elle, is that really you?"

"I take it I accomplished my mission of being unrecognizable then," Elle laughed as she slid onto the soft leather seats.

"Yes, ma'am. That's for sure. Do you need me to come in and play bodyguard? You're going to have a hard time keeping the riff-raff away tonight."

Elle smiled — most of that riff-raff was paying $25,000 a head to attend tonight. "No thanks. Although my mother would be delighted if it ever came to that."

"I'm surprised she's not going to be there to casually whisper into the ears of all the single men that they should ask you to dance. Not that they'll need any prompting. In that dress, you'll be attracting them for reasons other than being a powerful woman. They'll be tripping over their tongues to get to you." Finn paused before closing the door. "Are you sure you don't want me to go with you?"

Elle laughed, "I'm sure. Thanks, Finn. I'm looking forward to embracing my anonymity, and I think having you glare at every man asking me to dance may give away my identity. But I do appreciate you looking out for me."

Finn gave her a wink and closed the door. Elle sank into the comfortable seat as Finn drove toward the ball. Tonight she was going to be free.

Chapter Two

Although this Christmas ball caused him pain, Drake Charles also knew firsthand how much it could help people. His family had buried his younger sister, Delilah, just one week before Drake received his college acceptance letter. Delilah had been diagnosed with leukemia at the age of thirteen. They had tried everything to save her. On her fifteenth birthday, Delilah had blown out her candles and had spent a wonderful day with the family in her room at Children's Hospital. Their parents had kissed her good-bye and had gone to get the car while Drake had stayed with her.

"You're going to get in, you know. You're the smartest guy I know. And that's saying a lot—look where I live. Doctors everywhere," Delilah had teased through a coughing fit.

"I don't know. It'll be a bunch of trust-fund brats and me. Maybe I'll just stay here and go to State."

"Don't let anything intimidate you, Drake. You're meant for great things. More than that, you're a good person. When you make it, you'll change the world for the better. Now, kiss your sister good-bye and go conquer the world."

Drake had leaned down and kissed her good-night. Looking back, it had been clear she'd known she wouldn't make it to morning. She died in her sleep three hours later.

Honoring his sister's last wish, he'd accepted the scholarship to the small elite college in Massachusetts and had headed off to school a couple months later. Drake's mother had cried when he'd accepted the scholarship. His father had slapped him on the back and had bought a ten-dollar bottle of wine to celebrate. It'd been the first happy news his blue-collar family had received in the past two years.

When Drake had arrived at college, one of the first people he'd met was Chip Aubrey. He and Chip had had their issues. Chip had been exactly the kind of trust-fund brat Drake had worried about. But they'd become friends after a night that had begun with two bloody noses and had ended with an empty bottle of bourbon. When Drake had come up with an idea for new technology that blended third-party apps into smartphone operating systems with far better security, it'd been Chip's family's bank that had given him the small business loan to get up and running.

As soon as his enhanced security measures had been developed, tech companies had practically knocked each other over beating a path to his door. Overnight he had become one of the wealthiest men in the world at the age of twenty.

Reporters had swarmed his house and invaded his life, and he had basked in it. Until the reporters had found out about his sister. They'd asked mercilessly about his sister, her death, and his feelings about it. It'd caused Drake to shut down. The raw pain of the constant reminder had been enough to make him hate reporters. He'd returned his Lamborghini and had bought a 4-Runner. He'd ditched the two-thousand-dollar suits for jeans and a baseball cap. For a year he had done no public relations. His PR department had released all notifications of new products and had performed all interviews.

Slowly, he'd begun to emerge in public again but had done his best to stay under the radar of journalists. When he hadn't appeared to reclaim the spotlight, people had become more interested in making up rumors. He'd decided he could live with that. It had allowed him to spend time with his family, volunteer at the hospital, and lead a more normal life. Unfortunately, dating would never be normal. There were too many socialites out there who only cared about yachts, vacations to St. Bart's, and the size of the diamonds on their fingers.

That was why he had made this annual ball a masquerade. The tickets had been priced so high that they paid for most of the hospital staff and their families to attend for free. Deep down, he had a wish to meet a normal woman. One who didn't know how much money he had. One who enjoyed talking to him for the sake of good conversation. It sounded silly and he knew that. But even as his hope had faded over time, he'd kept hosting the ball, wishing to find that spark.

That spark was definitely not coming from the curvy bottle-blonde in front of him. Drake stood quietly behind her, clenching his jaw as he listened to Missy Jenner talk to her date, who happened to be his college friend, Chip Aubrey. In fact, to grab his attention, he would need someone quite the opposite of Missy, whose rich daddy bought, and continued to fund, his daughter's makeup company.

"I heard he isn't even here. They say it's some medical condition that has him bedridden," Missy Jenner said with an unmistakable hint of judgment.

"Sugarbear, I don't think so. I know Drake from college

and he was a very healthy and athletic guy. I don't know where these silly rumors start, but Drake Charles is not some elderly invalid."

Drake took a sip of champagne as he made a mental note to call Chip for a basketball game soon. Then he'd introduce him to his secretary — a sweet single mother with a solid head on her shoulders.

Elle's cell phone rang just a couple blocks out from the charity ball. She didn't need to look at it to know who it was. "Hello, Mother."

"Good evening, dear. Are you on your way to the ball?"

"You know I am, Mother," Elle sighed. Her mother still liked to pretend she was calling just to talk.

"Oh, I daresay the ball will be full of men looking handsome in their tuxedos. Maybe you'll even dance a time or two. I can't wait to hear about it in the morning." And there it was. The real reason her mother called.

"Yes, Mother. I'm sure there will be lots of people there."

"Just enjoy yourself, that's all I'm saying. It wouldn't hurt to find a guy, you know. You're too sweet and lovable to be without a good man. Go find that true love your father and I had."

"Thank you, Mom. I'll try to dance a time or two. See you in the morning for a marathon Christmas cookie baking session." Elle hung up the phone and looked out at the lights.

She didn't want to tell her mother, but she had already decided to enjoy herself. She wished to meet a dark, mysterious man who would whisk her away from reality for one night. Her last relationship had ended almost a year ago. They'd dated for three months and she'd thought it was going well. However, he'd begun dropping hints on their last date. But not the kind of hints she had hoped for. No, it had been more like, "Elle, while you have your board meeting this weekend, I would sure love to take my buddies to Aspen. Can I borrow the G5 and maybe you could spot me fifty Gs to show them a good time?" It was then she'd realized she was only a piggy bank to him.

It had ruined her confidence and her already shaky trust in men. Were they just trying to get to know her because she was rich? Or were they corporate spies? After dating Chord she had learned her lesson. It was hard to relax and be herself around men. She wanted to be the woman who curled up at home and watched movies in her bunny slippers while eating chocolate ice cream straight from the carton. She was tough enough at work every day—she didn't want to be that way in a relationship, too. That's why she was dreaming tonight. Dreaming of a man to give her enough memories to sustain her for another year of sitting alone on the couch at night.

Elle looked out the window as the limo came to a stop. The museum was lit up like Christmas against the dark night sky.

"We're here. I'm going to hop over to the mall and do some last-minute Christmas shopping. If I don't hear from you sooner, I'll meet you right here at one-thirty to take you back to the office," Finn told her as he held the door open.

"Thank you, Finn." Elle stepped out and smiled for the flashes from the photographers. They'd have fun trying to figure out who was who with everyone wearing full masks or a half-mask like she'd donned. Although, she was sure most of the guests would have gotten out of their cars without their masks just to make sure they were in the paper's society section.

She walked the red carpet and paused in front of the Drake Charles Foundation and Children's Hospital sign for her official photograph. She ignored the questions of who she was and just smiled before she went through the ornate glass doors and into the art museum. Beautiful masterpieces hung on the walls, and lights cast a warm glow upon the dancers below her. Elle took her time looking over the large crowd as she made her way down the set of white marble stairs. Groups of people stood on the perimeter of the large room talking as waiters walked among them passing out hors d'oeuvres and champagne. Mr. Charles certainly didn't spare any expense for this year's party.

Elle smiled as she stopped at the bottom of the stairs and watched the dancers. They were twirling around the dance floor while laughing and talking to their partners. She hoped someone would ask her to dance.

"Excuse me, Vivienne?"

Elle turned and looked down, way down, to the man standing next to her.

"Wrong person, sorry."

"My apologies. I'm Dr. Martin Brist, plastic surgeon. And who might you be?"

"If I told, it would defeat the purpose of a masquerade, wouldn't it?" Elle teased as she eyed the champagne tray making its way toward her. She silently prayed there would be some left when the waiter got to her. When she had dreamed of a guy talking to her and asking for a dance, it wasn't a man who was five-feet-two with a balding head and a potbelly, wearing a peacock mask. Elle smiled to herself and he puffed up, thinking the smile was for him, confirming her suspicions. He was quite literally a preening peacock tonight.

"Well, since I can't find Vivienne . . ."

No, don't do it, Elle mentally chanted as the man started stuttering. Then she saw him look up and smile. She followed his gaze and saw the mistletoe hanging above. Uh-oh.

"Excuse me. I want to catch someone before he leaves." Elle smiled politely and made a dash for the waiter with one last glass of champagne on his tray.

She reached for it with a grateful smile to the waiter. A hand closed around hers at the same time hers closed around the glass stem. "Oh!" Elle stepped back, but refused to let go of her hold on the last glass of champagne.

The hand was big and strong and attached to a very nice tuxedo-clad arm, which was attached to broad, muscular shoulders. Elle jerked her head up and was met with dark blue eyes behind a simple black mask that blended into black hair. His lips were full, his jaw strong, and there was no tell-tale ring around a particular finger. Elle fought the urge to shiver and melt all at the same time. Maybe her wish had been granted after all.

Chapter Three

Drake wasn't used to losing his cool, but as he looked down at the fiery redhead in front of him, he felt a primal urge like he'd never felt before. His hand closed tighter around hers, not wanting to lose the magic between them.

Beautiful green eyes shone through her mask, and he felt himself grow hot with desire. The pink dress clung to full breasts and rounded hips. A slit off to the side of her dress exposed a smooth leg all the way to her thigh. He found himself staring at it, willing it to fall open just a little more.

"I believe this is mine," she told him a little breathlessly. Apparently he wasn't the only one affected.

"Maybe we could share," Drake said with a suggestive smile. His voice was husky with the heady feeling of meeting someone he was instantly attracted to. He let go of the drink, thinking he suddenly didn't need it to survive the night. Instead his heart pounded as he took a step closer to the woman.

"Share? I don't think so. I'm not into sharing . . . anything." He felt a rush when she devoured him with her eyes. Oh, he was definitely intrigued now.

Elle took a sip of the champagne but couldn't feel the sweet bubbles tickling her mouth. Instead she only felt her body responding to the man standing in front of her.

"It looks like we have something in common. Once something is mine, I never share either." His deep voice lilted with a slight southern drawl that enveloped her. Suddenly she felt like a woman again. The way his eyes explored her body gave her a new sense of power. This is what she'd been seeking.

"I doubt you have a problem keeping what is yours. I wonder how you do it? You must teach me." Elle was shocked at the way her voice purred. She had no idea who she was, but she knew who she wasn't tonight. She decided to go for it.

He leaned his head back and laughed. "It would be my pleasure to teach you a great many things, my dear."

Elle felt her face flush and then moved closer to him as she saw a group of women eyeing the man she was talking to. The orchestra started a new song and she turned, brushing his shoulder as she looked at the dancers. Would he ask her to dance? Would he hold her tight against him as they glided along the floor?

"Are you here with anyone tonight?" he asked in the barest of whispers.

"No. There's no one special in my life right now." Suddenly she grew nervous. There hadn't been a ring but that didn't mean there wasn't a girlfriend or a fiancée. "Are you here with someone?"

"Yes. You." He grinned like a flirty teenager. "So, why did you come tonight?"

"My mother volunteers at the hospital. My family gets together every week for dinner and she always talks about the children she sees. I feel as if we're all a part of the place now. We all support it in any way we can."

Her mother had started volunteering after her father had passed away. It had given her a purpose again. She read to the children at the hospital, helped the nurses and the families, and always brought chocolate for the kids who could have it.

"That's nice of your family. Is your mother your date tonight?"

"No. She's getting the house ready for Christmas. Tomorrow, on Christmas Eve, my brother, two sisters, and I will report to the house bright and early to make cookies and decorate the tree. Then we stay in our old rooms until after Christmas." Elle smiled as she was filled with happy Christmas memories.

"That sounds lovely. My parents come to my house since I've . . . become older. There's nothing better than Mom's Christmas dinner, is there?"

Elle looked up into his eyes and saw the warmth in them as he talked about his family. There was something deeper to him than just a hot body and a sexy voice. It was that something that turned her on more than the flat stomach and mesmerizing eyes.

Drake looked down at the woman now by his side. Their shoulders touched occasionally as they watched the dance floor. He saw the men blatantly checking her out and moved closer to her to ward them off. It was strange, though; for all her talk, she didn't seem to notice the attention. It surprised him and pleased him greatly. She was no Missy Jenner.

He noticed a man nearby grab two glasses of champagne and head their way. It was time to stake his claim. The thought of anyone else touching this woman was unbearable.

He gently took her drink and set it on the table. "Shall we dance?" She smiled and nodded her head slowly.

Drake rested his hand on the small of her back and navigated her through the crowd and onto the dance floor. He held up his hand and she softly placed hers in it. Desire shot through him, knowing she was feeling what he was: nervous, enchanted, and determined all at once.

He enclosed her hand in his and wrapped his other around her back, resting it slightly lower than normal. Drake felt the curve of her bottom and pressed her closer to him. He knew she could feel his arousal by the way her cheeks flushed below her mask and her eyes darkened.

Elle glided along the floor with him leading the way. Drake couldn't take his eyes off hers. "You're a wonderful dancer," he leaned down to whisper in her ear.

"Thanks. My mom again. She made all of us take dance classes. What can I say?" Elle shrugged as she kept her eyes on his.

He felt her fingers gently tease the nape of his neck. The action emboldened him as he ran his fingers slowly down her spine.

"My family is kinda quirky," she stated with a smile.

"They sound delightful. What about your father?" Drake felt her momentarily stiffen and then relax.

"He passed away from a heart attack eight years ago. That's when my mother decided we, as a family, needed to do a weekly activity together. We did a new one every year. First it was dance lessons and then it was art classes. Let me tell you, drawing a naked man while sitting next to your mother is rather uncomfortable."

Drake laughed at the expression on her face.

"And then there was knitting, which was when my brother drew the line and moved back to Europe. But not before naming basketball as the next year's activity. Sadly, my mother at sixty-one can outshoot my youngest sister. Then there were photography, pottery, and cooking classes."

Drake chuckled. It sounded wonderful. He was close to his parents, too, but they were happily enjoying retirement in Key West. Although they were visiting more and more often. "That's seven. What are you doing this year?"

Elle hesitated. It didn't seem like he was making fun of her. Her mother may be a pain in the butt, but she was her pain in the butt. In fact, no one knew about their weekly classes followed by a family dinner. She was strangely protective of it, yet she was so comfortable talking to him that she hadn't even realized she'd told him about her family's most treasured time together.

"Fencing."

"With swords?" His lips quirked, but his eyes shone with good humor.

Elle couldn't help but laugh. "Yes, with swords. After the embarrassment with basketball, my sister wanted to redeem herself. She loves historical romance novels and finds it romantic when a man duels to defend his lady's honor. So when it was her turn to choose the activity, she chose fencing."

"Can she beat your mother?"

"It's a draw. Luckily they're good sports about it and it's actually funny."

"Which activities did you pick?"

"Art and photography."

"Why'd you choose those?"

Elle paused as she considered her answer. Talking to him was so easy, but tonight was about freedom and she wanted to protect her identity. "I wanted to be able to do something artistic because it's so different from my day-to-day life."

"I just met you, but I can picture you painting or walking the streets looking for new angles to photograph." He brought his lips to her ear and whispered, "It's very sexy."

Elle felt a shiver go down her spine as her body heated up. She also felt relief that he didn't press further. But then the music ended and they came to a stop. She gazed into his eyes waiting to see if he would suggest getting another drink or if he was going to say his good-byes. He glanced down at her but made no move to leave the dance floor with the other couples. Instead he kept her pressed against him as he waited for the next dance to begin.

Whoever this man was, he had given her enough memories to last at least one more year. She couldn't wait to see what would happen next. It was a Christmas miracle and she couldn't help wanting more.

Chapter Four

The music started again and the masked man swept Elle around the dance floor. Elle felt his fingers softly flex into her hip as he led her through another dance. His muscular thighs brushed purposely against her as they swayed across the floor, not allowing her a moment's reprieve from his presence. Not that she wanted it.

"Food?" he asked.

"Italian," they both said at the same time and laughed. So far they enjoyed the same movies, the same sports, and now the same foods. The only thing they differed on was books. He liked nonfiction and she enjoyed fiction.

"Childhood nickname?" he asked with a smile on his lips. Elle tried to keep up the smile, but she felt it slip at the memory. "I'm sorry. You don't have to answer that if you don't want to."

"No. It's okay. I don't have a childhood nickname, but my father called all of us his Lyra, as in the five-star constellation in the shape of the harp." Elle laughed at his confused look and then felt the sad memory turn to a happy one. It was a story her father loved to tell. "In the mythical story, Orpheus carried a harp and traveled to the underworld to rescue his true love. My father found comfort in it as he was forced to leave us for years in order to provide for the family. He always said that he'd find the brightest star in the harp and think of my mother back home singing to his four kids.

"Every night we'd look up into the sky to try to find Lyra, hoping our father was looking at it, too. It kept us all connected. When my father finally came home, my mother had a harp pin made and gave it to him. He wore it every day for the rest of his life." Elle smiled at the memory. In fact, the logo for Simpson Global had a harp on it as well, but it was so subtle that most people didn't notice it.

"That's so much better than mine. Mine was just embarrassing." He sighed and Elle snickered. What could it be? "It was Huggy Bear."

Elle tried not to laugh, but she couldn't stifle it. It bubbled up from her toes and she tossed her head back and laughed before she could stop herself. "Oh, I'm so sorry. I shouldn't laugh." She buried her head on his shoulder and laughed even more.

"I'm used to it. My mom still breaks out that gem every now and then. I was a very chubby baby, and women couldn't help but hug me when they saw me. What do you think? Do you find it impossible not to hug me?"

Elle stopped laughing as she realized she was wrapped around him. She looked up and the laughter started all over again. "Apparently your nickname still suits you. Okay, my turn. Stupidest thing you did as a kid?" Elle asked.

"When I was seven, I jumped off the roof of our small house with a bed sheet wrapped around my shoulders, thinking I could fly. I sadly realized I did not possess superpowers later that day as I sat in the hospital with a broken leg." He smiled and Elle licked her lips. She'd been staring into his eyes and watching his mouth move while he talked. And now all she wanted was to lean forward and kiss him. Even though she was being free tonight, she didn't think she could make the first move. Deep down she was just too nervous.

"What about you? I bet you didn't do anything stupid. You seem like you would have been the perfect well-behaved child," he said, bringing her eyes back to his.

"That was not the case," she said shaking her head. "As I told you, I have an older brother. Now, my older brother was always doing something stupid. He was probably the kid next to you in the hospital. But, he had taken up skateboarding and had been bragging to me about how there were no girls at the skateboard park because girls couldn't do it. It was a boy thing. Even at nine, I didn't like being told that. I still don't. So I locked him in his room, stole his skateboard, and ran to the park.

"My brother, being a complete bad boy, knew how to unlock the door and was chasing close behind me. I made it to the big ramp before he could shout for me to stop. I looked at him, stuck out my tongue, and hopped on," Elle said as she gave her head a little shake. Unfortunately or fortunately, depending on how you look at it, she still did that today. If they told her a woman couldn't run a company like Simpson Global, then she'd jump in with her tongue sticking out until the company was a huge success. She didn't like being told she couldn't do anything simply because she was a woman.

"And how did you do?"

"I hung on for dear life but refused to scream. I nailed it. My brother was eating crow, but then as I was skating home with him I hit a rock and face-planted. That's what this little scar on my chin is from." Elle lifted her chin to show the scar and felt a jolt as he leaned forward and placed his warm lips on it.

"It's adorable."

"What's your take on women skateboarders?" Elle asked a little breathlessly.

"They're hot. I like women who aren't confined by the norms. They're so much more exciting."

Elle breathed in sharply when he pulled her tightly against him, letting her feel just how excited he truly was. Her pulse quickened and she closed her eyes when he leaned forward to place a feather-light kiss on her cheek.

"I like women who are smart, compassionate, and have no problem asserting themselves." He kissed his way up to her ear and Elle tightened her hold on his shoulder.

"And sexy, of course," Elle said with a wink.

"If she's those things, then she's already sexy. You can be a knockout in that dress. But if you only wanted to talk jobs, money, and social standing, then you wouldn't be sexy. Now, the girl who refuses to back down—that is sexy."

Elle leaned closer to him as they danced. His hand moved back to the top of her bottom and his lips pressed sweet kisses to her neck. She was just about to fall under his spell when the music stopped and a man approached them.

Drake saw his assistant approaching and narrowed his eyes. But Phillip was too busy saying hello to the people he was passing to notice the cold stare Drake was giving him. Phillip couldn't meet this woman or he'd blow the insane connection they shared.

"Excuse me one second, my dear. I see someone I must talk to. Will you be here when I get back?"

"I guess you'll have to find out." He heard the laughter in her voice, but he also saw the men eyeing her with interest.

"I promise—you won't be sorry if you wait for me. It will only take a second." He swiftly leaned forward, brushing his lips against hers. When she leaned forward to complete the kiss, he stepped back and gave her a wink. Hopefully, that would keep her waiting. God knows it was enough to have him rushing through the crowd and grabbing his assistant.

"Drake," Phillip said, surprised.

"Shh. I don't want anyone knowing it's me."

Phillip rolled his eyes. "I don't understand your aversion to crowds. This is a great party."

"I know. It's not that." Drake cast a glance to where she stood talking to one of the men who had wasted no time filling his spot. "It's that woman. She's amazing and she has no idea who I am. We're talking and sharing. There's something there, I tell you."

"Really?" Drake had known Phillip since he was a kid. They had grown up on the same block and went to the same schools. Drake started his own company and realized he couldn't do everything himself. Phillip had told him he'd lost his job as a mechanic. He talked too much to the clients. Drake had hired him on the spot. He needed someone like that to make up for his own social awkwardness. Drake's inability to schmooze was his one big weakness.

"Really. I can't make that speech. You have to do it." Drake squeezed Phillip's shoulder in encouragement.

"What? It's your foundation. Who is she? Is she worth it?"

"I don't know. She hasn't told me her name either. But yes, she's worth it."

"I've never seen you lovesick before," he joked. "I'll do it. But you totally owe me."

"Yes, I do. Dr. Voss is too caught up in appearances and won't be wearing his hearing aids or his glasses. Just be me. They'll never know. Then get lost in the crowd and become Phillip again." Phillip nodded and headed for the stairs. Drake should feel bad, but, sadly, his assistant and friend had done this for him a number of times when Drake had locked himself in their research lab for weeks at a time finalizing new products.

Drake grabbed two glasses of champagne and hurried back to the woman's side. As he approached her from behind, he got a good look at the perfectly round butt he had been feeling the top of earlier. Just as he thought—no panties. This knowledge had him trying to control his arousal. It was a battle he was losing.

"Here you go, sweetheart," he said possessively as he handed her a drink and stepped closer to wrap his arm around her. He'd never been this way with a woman before, but he couldn't help himself. He wanted her all to himself.

"Thank you." She smiled up at him with amusement. He was making a fool of himself, but he didn't care. "This is Bob Michaels, president of International Media Group. He was just telling me how his media conglomerate made their first billion this year." She turned her head so only Drake could see her and rolled her eyes.

"Wow. Congratulations, Bob. The first billion is special. By the time you get to the fourth or fifth, it just gets repetitive. So enjoy it now. Excuse us, I owe this beautiful woman a tour of the Renoir exhibit."

She smiled and gave her head a slight nod as he escorted her past Bob. Bob was a smart man, but Drake knew he also had a habit of settling out-of-court for sexual harassment charges made by various secretaries.

"You're so bad. But I loved it. I couldn't think of anything to say. My mother raised me with manners. Bank accounts, religion, and politics were never talked about with guests. Now, get the family together and we can solve all of the world's problems."

He loved the light lilt to her voice as she laughed. Drake led her toward the back of the room, away from those gathering up close for what was supposed to be his speech. Their champagne glasses were now empty as they handed them to a waiter. He was about to slip out of the room when Dr. Voss stepped up to the microphone.

"Good evening, ladies and gentlemen. I'm Dr. Josiah Voss, the president of Children's Hospital, and I can't thank you enough for your generosity tonight."

"Oh, maybe we'll get to see the mysterious Drake Charles," she whispered to him as she stopped to look at the stage.

"Why are you interested in him?" Drake held his breath, hoping to avoid disappointment.

"Nothing of importance." He looked down at her and saw her nibble at her lip. She was lying.

"No reason? Come on, that can't be true."

"My brother thinks very highly of him and gave me an idea. It's just a business thing, and if there's one thing I don't want to do tonight, it's talk business."

"I couldn't agree with you more. I've heard he's very rich."

"Well, I'd hope so or he wouldn't be a very good businessman to have blown all that money he got from his Smartphone technology. Oh, there he is. Too bad I can't really see what he looks like from way back here." He looked down and saw her straining to get a view of the fake

Drake Charles.

"Good evening," Phillip called out to the crowd. Drake's speech for tonight would take twenty seconds to give. He hoped Phillip stuck to it. "Tonight we've raised six million dollars for Children's Hospital." He paused for the applause. "I appreciate your kindness and your generosity. Now drink all the champagne. You've definitely earned it." As the crowd laughed, Phillip stepped down from the stage and was promptly swamped by people.

Drake was relieved Phillip had stuck to his notes. When the music started, he slipped his arm around the woman and, once again, silently thanked Phillip. He owed him big time. There was something magical in the air tonight and he wanted to see where it took him. He knew when the night ended, he might not be able to give her up.

Chapter Five

Elle didn't want the night to end. She had been lost in her own fantasy with her dream man and wasn't ready to come back to reality. When he pulled her near him and started to slowly dance on the back edge of the dance floor, all thoughts of her life and responsibilities left her mind.

Instead of dancing the steps, they swayed together as he ran his strong hands up and down her back. He spun her and dropped his hand lower, cupping her bottom and giving it a squeeze as he kissed her neck. Elle wanted to moan, but the people who were whirling around them on the dance floor would surely hear her.

"You're so beautiful," he murmured as his lips worked their way up to her ear. His tongue traced the delicate shell before nipping at her earlobe. "Look up. Mistletoe."

"We can't break tradition now, can we?" Elle said with a grin.

She wrapped her arms around his neck as she tilted her head, giving him access to her lips. Elle shivered with pleasure and he tightened his hold on her. She felt his hardness pressing against her and grew warm in response. Unable to stop herself, she rubbed against him as his lips descended onto hers. His tongue caressed hers, leaving her breathless. Pulling away, their gazes locked and Elle saw his desire. And then he shot her a wicked smile that had her heart pounding.

Looking around the crowded room, she saw only a few people in the hallway leading to the Renoir exhibit. She looked back to him and nodded in the direction. Words were unnecessary. Without a doubt, she was going after what she wanted tonight. And what she wanted was him.

Drake's breath caught the second she rubbed against him. The need to be inside her was almost painful. When she gave him the look and nodded toward the exhibit, he had to restrain himself from dragging her down the hall. Instead, he laced his fingers with hers as they strolled across the marbled hall toward the exhibit. They passed other couples returning from the brightly lit gallery that held the prized Renoir paintings.

They stopped to admire a painting and when no one was looking, he hurried her through a set of black drapes hiding the exit and into a darkened hallway off the gallery room.

"Where are we going?" she whispered, her voice full of excitement.

"There's a small atrium with a glass ceiling just around the corner." Drake looked around and pushed open the doors. When no alarms went off, he led her through the door and walked into the small courtyard filled with plants. It had a small water fountain and two benches. Small white lights cast a magical glow around the room.

She twirled around and looked up at the night sky above them. "Shall we dance?" Drake asked as he gave her an elegant bow.

She laughed and he grasped her hand. His body was strumming with desire, but he willed himself to slow the pace. With no words, he led her in a dance around the fountain. He let his hands explore her body as they moved to the music in their heads. He felt the curve of her hip and the soft swell of her breasts as he ran his hands up and down her sides.

"I've never wanted someone as much as I want you," Drake confessed to her before he claimed her lips. She opened her mouth to respond and his tongue dipped in to taste her. Her hands tightened on the lapels of his tuxedo as his kiss deepened.

He dropped his hands to clasp her bottom. She wiggled closer to him and pressed against his hard length. Drake fought for control, but he knew it was a lost cause.

Elle's heart was pounding. Oh God. She was going to do this. Elle Simpson, Little Miss Proper, was going to have a one-night stand in a cute little courtyard tucked away but not too far from a roomful of people. Wearing the mask gave her a wild sense of freedom. As she rubbed herself against his unmistakable erection, she felt empowered. She had done that. Not her money, not her power—just the woman she was.

His hands were at her breasts, cupping them, caressing them. He traced her nipple with his finger before pinching and rolling it between his thumb and finger. Elle gave up any pretenses of slow seduction. She wanted him naked. Now.

She loosened his bow tie and started unbuttoning his shirt in a haze of passion. He was doing things to her that had her flushed from head to toe. But then she felt the air against her bottom. As one of his hands massaged her breast, the other had found the zipper to her dress.

Elle had exposed his smooth, defined chest when he

unfastened the necklace at the top of her dress, causing the two swaths of fabric to fall to her waist, baring her breasts to him. With one finger, he pushed the fabric at her waist and the dress pooled at her feet.

"You're perfect. A walking dream come true," his graveled voice said, his mouth coming down on hers with raw hunger. Their tongues sparred as his hands explored her naked body.

Elle grew wet with need as his fingers danced along the top of her thighs. She could no longer stand it. She had to feel him right this instant. She quickly discarded his shirt and ran her fingers over the ridges of his abs before feeling his erection through his pants.

"Off. Now," she ordered.

"Yes, ma'am. Your wish is my command." He had no idea, she thought. He, too, was a walking, talking dream and she was about to pinch his perfect behind to find out if he was real.

He quickly kicked off his shoes and unfastened his pants while he kept his mouth on hers. Elle became daring as she sucked his tongue and elicited a ragged moan from him. As soon as he was free, she wrapped her hand around his shaft and caressed it before slipping on the condom he handed her. He moved his mouth to her breast and pulled her taut nipple into his mouth. His fingers slid to her center and she lost what little control she had.

As if reading her mind, he moved her toward the bench. Taking a seat he pulled her to him. She straddled him, feeling his hard head probing her wet entrance. In one quick motion, she took him inside her.

"Oh, God. You feel better than anything I could have dreamed of," he said as he grabbed her hips, bringing her down on him again and again as he thrust inside her.

Elle thought about responding, but no words would come. She whimpered her pleasure as she tossed back her head. He cupped a bouncing breast, bringing her nipple to his mouth as she rode him. Pleasure shot through her body as she moved faster and faster upon his hardened length. He scraped her nipple gently with his teeth and the rolling waves overtook her. She shattered, screaming her pleasure into the night sky.

Seconds later, she felt him stiffen underneath her, his hands gripping her hips as he ground into her one last time.

"That was . . . I don't know what that was, but . . . it was amazing," he whispered as he pushed back a loose strand of hair that had gotten tangled in her mask.

Elle agreed with a nod of her head, not being able to find the words to express what had happened. She lingered a moment before leaning forward and resting her head on his chest with a smile. His fingers ran lazily up and down her spine as they sat quietly together in the courtyard trying to regain their breaths.

"I think the time has come to truly bare all." He reached up to his mask at the same time a loud ringing broke the tranquility of the courtyard.

Chapter Six

"**O**h my gosh . . . what time is it?" Elle scrambled off his naked body and grabbed her purse.

"I don't know. It's probably a couple hours past midnight. How about breakfast after this party breaks up?" Elle was too busy fumbling for her phone to answer.

"Hello?" she spoke into the phone.

"Elle, are you all right? Did something happen?" she heard Finn asking.

"I'm fine, why? What time is it?" she asked, looking around for her clothes.

"It's ten minutes until two. You're twenty minutes late and you're going to miss your conference call with the Swiss bankers if you don't get your butt out here right now."

"Oh no, I'll be there in just a second." Elle hung up the phone and tossed it on the bench as she tugged on her dress. She reached behind to grab the zipper. "Can you get this?" She lifted her hair and turned her back to her naked dream. Reality had just called and shattered her fantasy.

"I guess that means no to breakfast?" he asked with good humor as he fastened the top of her dress.

She shoved her breasts back into place and slipped her feet back into her heels. "Sorry. The real world called and

I'm needed." She leaned down and took one last kiss. She hated to leave but if she didn't run out and leave him right this instant, she was going to blow a huge deal. With regret, she turned and ran back into the gallery as fast as she could.

Elle raced down the corridor and over the dance floor. People stared at her, but she didn't care. She pushed the heavy glass door open and rushed onto the sidewalk. She looked around wildly for Finn. She heard a sharp whistle and turned to see him half a block down the street. She picked up her dress and ran.

"Come on. It's almost two. Haul ass, boss," Finn yelled as he held the door open for her.

"Get the car started," she shouted back between alternately gasping for air and cursing her high heels.

Finn nodded, jumped into the driver's seat, and started the car just as she leaped into the backseat and slammed the door closed. Tires squealed, horns honked, and the big limo shot out into the street, tossing her around on the seat.

"Looks like someone had a good night," Finn teased from the front seat.

Elle flushed. Could he tell she'd just had the most mind-blowing sex ever with the man of her dreams? "What do you mean?" she tried to ask innocently.

Finn laughed as he took a corner so fast that it sent her sailing to the other side of the limo. "Only that your hair is a mess and your shoes are on the wrong feet."

Elle looked down at her feet. This was so much more embarrassing than being caught with her bunny slippers on.

Drake sat stunned. The woman of his dreams had just disappeared into the night. He panicked and nearly chased after her until he remembered his nakedness. Damn, he didn't even get her name. She had to be an on-call doctor the way she ran off. He had to find her before she left.

Drake shot to his feet and tugged on his pants. He slipped on his shoes, not even bothering with his socks. Instead he stuffed them into his pocket and went to work on his shirt. Getting it halfway buttoned was good enough, he thought, slinging on his jacket. He looked around to grab his bow tie and saw the small black phone sitting next to it on the bench. She'd left her phone.

He grabbed it and hurried through the thinning crowds as people made their way to their cars. Lines of limousines stretched down the street. But it was the one half a block away with the squealing tires that made his heart plummet. He'd lost her. He looked at the phone in his hand. It was the only lead to find the woman of his dreams.

Drake sat in his office and stared at the phone. He tried turning it on, but the battery was almost dead and it was password protected. Good thing he happened to have a lot of phones around. He went into the lab and found the right charger. He plugged it in and started trying to guess her password.

"Dammit." The most common passwords didn't work. He shouldn't be surprised. There was nothing common about this woman. He found a USB cord and connected the phone to his computer. It was time to get serious. There was no way he was going to lose this woman. He would find her no matter how long it took.

Elle gave Finn a quick kiss on his cheek and wished him a merry Christmas before punching the elevator button in the

secure parking garage below her building. She looked in her purse for her phone to check the time and froze. No phone. The elevator dinged and she hopped in, pressing the top floor.

She had to have left it in the courtyard. She'd have to call security and have them check. Crap. That phone had her life in it. At least her brother had talked her into putting a state-of-the-art security system in it. She knew no one would be able to hack it. She would go pick it up later.

The doors to the elevator opened and she hurried through the dark hallway maze to her office. She flipped on the lights and glanced at the clock. She had two minutes. She kicked off her shoes, untied her mask, and slipped out of her dress. She then grabbed some tissues to wash the makeup from around her eyes. She applied some light brown and beige eye shadow as her computer hooked up to the videoconference.

She pulled a cream-colored blouse out of the closet and slipped it on. Her computer started beeping, indicating an incoming videoconference call. She grabbed a blazer and buttoned it up. Her bare bottom sat down in the leather chair by the third ring. Elle tucked her hair back and pressed Accept.

"*Grüezi mitenand,*" she said in Swiss German as the bank's board of directors appeared. The men looking back at her all said hello as well, and they got to work.

Elle smiled and said good-bye to the group of bankers all heading home for Christmas. The three-hour conference call had wiped her out. Further, she struggled for the first time in her life to pay attention. She'd be listening to someone and the image of looking down at her masked-man's face as she sat naked upon him took over her mind.

She wished she could kick herself as she slipped on her panties and a pair of jeans. She'd left the only man she'd had crazy chemistry with sitting naked on a bench. One thing she knew for sure—he wasn't out for her money. Add to that the fact that she instantly trusted him, and the feeling of being in his arms made her decide with surety that she couldn't settle for one-night stands. She wanted the rest of her life filled with nights like that. The sadness that wrapped her like a blanket tightened. She'd met the *one* and she'd never see him again.

With tears trickling down her face, she wrapped up the Swiss bank deal, made her way to her car, and drove forty-five minutes to her mother's house.

Drake cursed and sat back in his chair. Who was this woman? She had top-of-the-line security on her phone that most people didn't even know about. How did he know that? He'd invented the damn thing. The good news was he could hack it. The bad news, it was going to take a while and he didn't have the time now. He was due at Children's Hospital to hand out presents. His perfect woman's identity had to wait a bit longer.

Chapter Seven

Elle slammed the reindeer cookie cutter down and viciously yanked the extra dough from around it. Her mother, brother, and sisters all stopped to stare at her.

"Whoa. Put the reindeer down gently and step away from Santa," her brother said in mock seriousness.

"I thought it would get better after she took that long nap this morning, but she's been this way all afternoon," her mother told her siblings, as if Elle wasn't standing right in the middle of them.

"What's up, Elle? Did the business deal with the Swiss not go well?" Bree asked, sprinkling a cookie.

"It was fine. The papers are all signed and express-mailed to the government agencies. The deal closed without a hitch," Elle told them as she stabbed the reindeer back into the dough.

"Did something happen at the dance then? Oh no," Allegra cried, "please, tell me that horrid man from that financial service company didn't find you. You know, the one we had thought about buying out?" Allegra turned to their mother. "He's been sending her flowers at the office."

"We have to remember how blessed we are. Although, I do wish you all had been of an age to be married before we became so blessed. I worry all the time about my babies being taken advantage of," her mother said worriedly as she poured some more flour into the mixer.

"I wouldn't mind being taken advantage of," Reid joked as he wiggled his eyebrows.

"I especially mean you, young man," their mother said without looking up from the mixer.

Elle grinned. Her brother was thirty-five, but their mother still talked to him as if he were thirteen.

"I want grandbabies, but not by some woman who tricked you into it. I just wish you all could find the true love that your father and I shared. You need to slow down, stop working so much, and get out there to enjoy life. Take risks, fall in love, get married, and give me grandbabies."

Elle and her sisters rolled their eyes while Reid looked distinctively pale at the idea of settling down. But, for as much as Elle laughed with her sisters, she had found what her mother wished for. She had taken a risk last night and had fallen in love—she stabbed the reindeer again—but she'd messed it all up. She didn't find out who he was and now her happily-ever-after would never come true.

"Did you get a chance to meet Drake Charles last night? He's such a wonderful man. So compassionate," her mother told them.

"Drake and Margaret sitting in a tree, K-I-S-S—" Allegra began to sing before their mother, Margaret, hit her in the face with a well-aimed dusting of flour.

"Oh, please," her mother laughed as Allegra wiped the flour off.

"See. Mom has a crush on the elusive Mr. Charles," Allegra teased.

"You'd have a crush, too, if you met him. He's the type of man you should be looking for," she informed her daughters.

"I'm not going to marry some old, reclusive man, Mom. Sorry," Elle complained as she handed the reindeer to her brother who put it on a cookie sheet.

"He's not a recluse. He leaves his house all the time. He owns that big building on the same street as your offices. You know the one, just two blocks down. He goes to work there every day. Once a week he stops by the hospital to read to the kids. And once a month he brings them a toy or a book. Just because he avoids extra attention doesn't mean he's a recluse," her mom said passionately.

But it didn't matter to Elle. The thought of dating anyone right now put a bad taste in her mouth. There was only one man she wanted in her life and kooky Drake Charles was not the one.

Drake knocked on the hospital door decorated with princess stickers. Entering the room, he handed his last wrapped package to the little girl inside. Her parents sat smiling beside her bed while they held hands.

Tara was just ten years old and fighting cancer. She's lost her hair but refused a wig. She was determined to beat it and she was showing positive signs so far.

"Merry Christmas, Tara. Hi, Dina. Grant." He nodded to her parents and placed the box on Tara's bed. "I don't know, Tara. I've been hearing how you've been sneaking into the nurses' lounge at night and eating ice cream. You might be moved to the naughty list."

The little girl grinned, not looking guilty at all. "Well, they said to take it one day at a time. I'm just choosing to take it one ice cream at a time. If you don't go after what you really want, there's no guarantee you'll be around to get it tomorrow."

Truer words had never been spoken. And the only *want*

he could think of was the woman from last night. He didn't care if it involved hacking a phone or hunting her down by any other means. He was going to find her. "How old are you again? I might need to take this back and get you a briefcase so you can take over the world."

"I'm ready, but my body isn't yet. It will be soon, though." She smiled and her rounded face lit up. Drake raised an eyebrow questioningly.

"We got the latest tests back. She's in remission," Dina said with tears of joy welling in her eyes.

"I get to go home in a couple weeks. Isn't that fantastic? I haven't been home in three months," Tara said excitedly.

"Oh, that's fantastic." Drake gave the girl a hug and shook her parents' hands. When Tara had been admitted three months ago, the outlook for remission was bleak and Tara had been given a short time to live. Grant's brother was a match for a bone marrow transplant, and after two rounds of chemo and radiation, Tara had undergone the procedure. So far, she was now producing healthy cells.

"Here. Open your Christmas gift. Although it seems Santa already gave you something even better this year."

Tara tore open her gift with glee and placed the big ribbon on Drake's head. She opened the box and pulled out a beautiful princess doll. Inside were matching pajamas, dresses, and tiaras for the doll and Tara.

"This is so cool! Thanks, Drake." Tara put on the tiara and hugged her doll.

"Now, when you go home, you're not going to forget me, are you? Remember, I have a college scholarship with your name on it." There was no doubt Tara was going to change the world.

"Mr. Charles, you've done so much for us. We'll never forget you." Dina hugged him and he felt almost complete.

He was just missing the redhead by his side to share this moment. Maybe she was even somewhere in the hospital now.

"Keep me updated. You all have my personal email. I want lots of pictures."

"You got it," Grant said as he shook Drake's hand.

"Merry Christmas." Drake smiled as he saw Dina take a seat on the bed to ooh and aah over the doll.

Now Drake had a mission. He looked around the hall and saw only a few nurses. They must be celebrating the holiday in the nurses' station. He made his way down the hall and into the back room where they were eating the desserts he'd brought.

"Caught y'all red-handed," Drake teased the six nurses taking their break.

"Mmm, these are delicious. You spoil us, Drake."

"I did it to butter y'all up. I need two things. First, does anyone know how much Tara's bill is? I know her mother works at a coffee shop and her father is in construction. They can't have that much money."

A nurse went to the computer and pulled it up. "Looks like they have insurance, but there's some things that aren't covered. It'll be close to twenty thousand by the time she leaves. You want to do the regular?"

"Yes. Just send me the bill." When Drake knew families were strapped for cash, he silently paid the bill while the families were left wondering why their accounts showed a zero balance. "Now, the second thing I need is to find the owner of this cell phone. A lady dropped it at the gala last night. She's about five feet six inches with red hair and green eyes. She's probably in her late twenties, early thirties. She told me her mother volunteers here and I think she might be a doctor."

"That would make her mother in her fifties or sixties," one of the nurses mumbled as Drake could see her thinking of all the volunteers.

"Unfortunately for you, that's the age range with the most volunteers. But I don't know of any redheaded women doctors that age here. Do you, Stella?"

"No. I sure don't. The only redhead on staff is a man. So, I think it's safe to say she's not a doctor here. And you're sure her mother volunteers here?" Nurse Stella asked.

"Positive." Drake nodded.

"Does she have any brothers or sisters? Does she have kids or is she an aunt?"

"Yes, she mentioned having sisters and maybe a brother. But she didn't say anything about kids," Drake told them.

One of the nurses in the back of the room snapped, "I know who it is. It has to be Margaret Simpson. She's here at least three times a week. She's one of our best volunteers and she's always joking about having to come here to make up for the fact she doesn't have any grandchildren of her own. She treats everyone here as if they were hers. The kids love her. You know her."

Drake tried to remember all the volunteers, but there were so many.

"That's right. And while her hair is kind of blond now, there are streaks of red in it. Goes by the nickname Retty," another nurse put in.

"Oh, I know who you're talking about. Thank you so much. You've been a big help," Drake said as he prepared to leave. How many Margaret Simpsons were in the Atlanta area?

"I'm surprised you don't know her oldest daughter,

Elle," a nurse in the back of the room said.

That had him stopping in his tracks. Elle—that name struck a chord for him. "Elle? Why would I know her? Is she a doctor here?"

"No. She's in big business like you. She's the CEO of Simpson Global. I guess you could have meant one of her sisters, Bree or Allegra. But I think Elle's the one with the golden red hair. Her sisters are more strawberry blond. Elle's a big supporter of Children's Hospital, too. She's the one who paid for the new MRI machine."

Drake stood rooted to the ground. Elle Simpson—business's most powerful woman and the woman on this month's *Business Weekly* magazine. He couldn't believe it. Although now that he thought about it, Phillip had said she was a fox when he placed the magazine on Drake's desk a couple of weeks ago. Her red hair had been pulled back and she'd been in a suit and had on minimal makeup: the standard executive getup. Strip that away and shake out her hair—yeah, he could see it, but there was no way she could be the owner of the phone. The owner of the phone was hot and passionate, not cold and ruthless as he'd heard Elle described. He'd just have to keep looking.

"Thank you, ladies. That may be the woman I talked to. I'll make sure to get this phone back to her. Merry Christmas." Drake flashed a half-hearted smile and walked from the room.

"That's not all he'll make sure she gets," one of the nurses said as the others giggled.

Elle Simpson. "I'll be damned," he muttered to himself as he rolled the idea around in his mind. No wonder she didn't want to talk business or money. She had just as much as he did and she was probably in the exact same situation as he was when it came to dating. He just couldn't believe the stiff CEO on the cover of *Business Weekly* was the same woman who stripped him down and made love to him on a bench. He could still feel her, taste her, and he responded instantly to the image of her breasts bouncing as she rode him. Drake stopped at his car and it seemed as if all the worry left him. Suddenly he was smiling. He just might have found her, but he needed to dig deeper to confirm it. It just seemed too out of character for the ruthless CEO.

Chapter Eight

D rake tried to find Elle's address while he drove to his house to meet his parents. Just like her phone, the information seemed as if it had been made purposely hard to get. Which it probably had been. Just like his address. But it was damned inconvenient right now.

However, he had found out with a well-placed phone call to Phillip, who knew everything about everyone, that Elle wasn't your typical woman. Her business portfolio was beyond impressive. Instead of folding when it had gotten tough, she had pulled in her family and had told them to do whatever they loved. As a result, Simpson Global had expanded in many different directions.

It was also evident that she was a mostly private person. While she attended some events and was featured in some magazines, she focused exclusively on business. Elle ferociously protected her personal life, especially after she had a very public breakup with a man when she first became CEO. According to Phillip, the man had been nothing but a corporate spy who went on a smear campaign in order to help facilitate what turned out to be a failed takeover.

Drake was impressed, though. She'd come out stronger and more respected than ever. Elle had not only prevented the takeover, she'd also managed to beat that competitor in several business deals the following year. She had made her point without ever going to the media, never complaining, never filing suit. Nope. She'd earned respect and had sent a clear message to anyone who dared to cross her again.

He knew about her business, but he really wanted to know *her*. Phillip had found articles where she had received numerous philanthropic awards. She'd never publicized herself like the politicians, celebrities, and other CEOs who took camera crews with them to a soup kitchen. No, Elle had gone in jeans and a T-shirt and the only evidence she had spent all this time helping others was some grainy photos taken by cell phones and the awards she had been nominated for. She spent time working with underprivileged youths, women in business, children, and animals. She enjoyed sports and her family was very close, just like his.

He looked at the clock in the car and stepped on the gas pedal. His parents were already at his home. His mother was probably fretting about overcooking the Christmas Eve turkey while his father was probably sprawled out on the couch watching any football game he could find. Even though the only thing he wanted to do was find out if Elle was the woman he had been with, it would have to wait.

He pressed one of the buttons on his rearview mirror and the large gate guarding the entrance to his house slid open. A tall stone fence lined the street with thick trees, blocking the view of the sprawling antebellum estate from passersby.

He had been comfortable in his small downtown apartment, but his mother and father had sold their house in Atlanta and had moved to the beach. They seemed to be coming home more and more frequently and staying with him for longer periods of time. Suddenly his apartment had seemed microscopic.

The day his mother had woken him while picking up his underwear in his room had been the last straw. He'd called a real estate agent, had given her a budget, and had told her the house had to have a kitchen big enough for them all to gather. Dinnertime was special while growing up and that tradition had continued. He had also told her the house had to be big enough for him to hide after said dinner to avoid his mother's constant reminder about not letting life pass him by. If the pattern of their visits continued, it would probably just get worse if he ever did get married and have kids. So, he had instructed the real estate agent to find a house with a separate guesthouse.

So far it had been working well. Both he and his parents felt independent and they weren't tripping over each other. But tonight, the night after the ball, he was going to be grilled. No matter how large his house, there would be no escaping it.

He parked his car in the garage and made his way to the kitchen, all the while daydreaming of Elle. The smells of Christmas Eve dinner floated through the air and mixed with the smell of the fresh evergreen tree in the nearby living room. His mother, fully outfitted with her own apron, stood guard over the turkey in the oven.

"Oh, thank heavens. What took you so long? The turkey would have been overcooked if you had been any later," Penny Charles clucked as she scolded him. The turkey would be perfect. The turkey had never been overcooked. Even when he was nineteen and was two hours late arriving from college, the turkey had been perfect.

"Merry Christmas, Mom." Drake ignored the clucking and wrapped his mother up in a hug that brought her off the ground, screaming to be put down. He'd started doing that to his mom when he hit six feet, towering almost a foot over her.

He'd inherited his height from his father, Steven, who was six-foot-one. "Son. Glad you're home. How were the kids?"

"Great. Tara will be released in a couple weeks."

"Oh, wonderful." Penny pulled the turkey out of the oven and Drake almost started drooling. "Now, tell us about the ball. Was it beautiful? Was it romantic?" She clapped her hands together before pulling out a giant knife.

"It was beautiful and everyone had a great time." Drake knew he did. He'd found Elle Simpson.

"If only you had a wife to share it with," Penny sighed as she prepared to cut the turkey.

Drake paused and thought about the night with Elle. It had been better than any night of his life because he was with her. Sure, there was hot sex, but the laughing and talking and dancing — all things he had hated to do with women prior to last night — had been wonderful.

"You know, Mom, you may be right about that." Drake snagged a pinch of stuffing and headed into the living room. All he heard was the clanging of the knife on the stone floor behind him and what might have been his mother fainting. But he had a very important phone call to make that couldn't wait.

Elle fluffed her pillow and flopped back down on it with a huff. She stared at the ceiling in hopes of finally falling asleep but knew it wouldn't happen. She was mad. She was livid. Worst of all? It was with herself.

She had fallen in love with a man, and what did she do? She'd run out leaving him naked and never even remembered to ask his name. His name. She had been so naïve in thinking she could have a one-night stand with a man like him. He was tall, handsome, kind, funny . . . Elle turned over, buried her head in her pillow, and screamed.

Slowly she raised her eyes from the pillow and looked at the red numbers on the clock. It was a little before midnight and it looked like sleep would not be coming for a while. Giving up the pretense, Elle swung her feet out of bed and pulled on the red silk robe draped over the chair before heading downstairs.

A light from the kitchen spilled onto the bottom of the stairs. She heard the sink turn off and wondered who was still awake. She walked into the kitchen and saw her mom, wearing the same fuzzy robe she'd had for twenty years, drying the last of the dirty dishes.

"You know, we have a dishwasher," Elle said as she snagged a Christmas cookie.

"And some things are done better when done by hand." Her mother placed her treasured china back into the cabinet and took a seat on the stool next to Elle. "So, what has you up so late?"

Elle pushed around the cookies and found a big star. "Just a problem I don't have the answer to and don't think I can solve." Her new idea was to eat all the cookies. Maybe she'd stop feeling so horrible.

"'Tis the season for miracles, sweetie. Why don't you ask Santa for help?" Her mother stood up, grabbed a reindeer cookie, and then kissed her forehead. "It's a couple of minutes before midnight. You still have time to make that Christmas wish. Good night."

Elle watched her mom disappear up the stairs and took another bite of her cookie. She knew her mother still saw her as a child sometimes, but making a wish to Santa Claus?

Elle rolled her eyes and got a plate to put cookies on.

She made herself a cup of hot chocolate and turned off the lights. The Christmas tree cast a warm glow across the living room and sparkled over the presents beneath it. Taking the plate of cookies and her drink, she sat on the comfy overstuffed chair looking at the tree and the childhood stockings her mother still hung.

She set her cup of hot chocolate and the plate of remaining cookies by the fireplace, walked over to the window, and looked up to the stars shining in the dark night sky. "Santa, all I want for Christmas is to find the man I've fallen in love with."

She closed her eyes and made a wish, too, just for extra luck. Then she quickly looked around and made sure none of her siblings were on the stairs. She felt foolish enough as it was, but she'd never hear the end of it if she were caught making a wish to Santa for a man.

Elle snapped her fingers. She got it. She'd hire a professional investigator to find Mr. Right. Feeling as if she'd done everything she could do on Christmas Eve, she headed upstairs for what little sleep she could get. She'd need it to pretend everything was all right in the morning and to settle the nervous excitement she felt. At least she had a game plan now.

Chapter Nine

Elle was peacefully dreaming of dancing with the black-haired, blue-eyed mystery man beneath the mistletoe when suddenly she felt as if she were falling. And not in love. She cracked her eyes and found her two sisters smiling down at her as they bounced on her bed.

It didn't matter that Bree was thirty-one and Allegra was twenty-nine. They loved Christmas and still woke Elle every Christmas to tell her Santa had come. When they'd grown older and had discovered there was no Santa Claus, they'd stayed up late trying to catch their mother, but never could. Somehow it just added to the magic of Christmas and Elle couldn't help but laugh now.

"I listened all night," Allegra laughed as she bounced again on the bed. "All I heard was Elle going down around eleven-thirty, but she was back before midnight. Do you think she pulled it off again?"

"I didn't hear Mom, either. It's embarrassing to admit at thirty-one, but I too stayed up to listen. Shall we see if there are more presents under the tree?" Bree tried to hide her excitement but failed.

Elle grabbed her pillow and threw it at them as she leaped off the bed. "I'm gonna beat you."

The three sisters tore out of the room and barreled over Reid as he made his way sleepily down the hall.

"I can't believe it." Elle slid to a stop behind Allegra and looked into the living room. The gifts had multiplied, the stockings were full, the hot chocolate had been drunk, and only crumbs were left on the cookie plate.

"She did it again. Twenty-five straight years we've tried to catch her and she's eluded us every time." Bree shook her head and went to grab a cup of coffee.

"Maybe you can't catch her because there really is a Santa Claus," Reid teased his sisters. They all smacked him as Bree held his cup of coffee hostage.

Elle laughed as they teased and joked with each other until their mother came downstairs, having been awoken by their noise. They all just laughed harder. Every year their mother and father had come downstairs exactly eighteen minutes after the kids ran downstairs. When Elle and her siblings were younger, they'd enjoyed those eighteen minutes of wonder by shaking gifts and trying to guess what they were. Now they just enjoyed the time with each other, dropping into the habits of old and acting like those same kids again.

"Oh, it looks like Santa came last night," Margaret said as she took her seat. "Are we going to open them?"

"Yes," her children all screamed as they took a seat on the floor and couch. Elle and her siblings laughed. They knew they were being childish, but this was what family was about—relaxing and being silly together. They were there for each other every day with serious and pressing business matters, but today was a day to have fun.

Elle tried not to laugh as her brother opened his last gift from her. He tore into the paper and ripped the tape off the box. He reached in and pulled out his gift.

"Fuzzy dice? Really, Elle?" Reid smiled. "They'll look

great hanging in my Aston Martin," he said dryly.

"I thought so, too. They'll really make your Vanquish hot." Elle giggled as the doorbell rang.

They all looked to the door, but her mother stood and turned to Allegra. "You get the door while I start on breakfast." Allegra jumped off the couch and disappeared into the entranceway as her mother softly hummed while walking to the kitchen.

Elle turned back toward her brother when she was hit with a pair of fuzzy dice. She promptly returned fire and then sent a wad of wrapping paper sailing through the air, hitting Bree smack in the middle of the face.

They all froze when they heard Allegra giggle from behind them. Elle's back was to her and she flushed at having been caught acting like a kid in front of company. "There is a man here from the art museum. He's saying something about a lost phone?"

Elle jumped up, not even worrying about her flannel pajamas with little snowmen on them. "My phone." She turned and came face to face with a handsome man in jeans and a red button-up shirt. Normally she'd find him attractive, but she was too excited to have recovered her phone. Besides, her mind and heart remained focused on the mystery man from the party.

"Merry Christmas, Miss. Could you turn the phone on for me to show me it's yours?" Elle eagerly grabbed the phone and entered her password. She paused as she looked at all the missed emails, feeling a slight panic that she may have missed something important.

"Nice dice you've got there," the man who delivered her phone said to Reid. Elle cocked her head. She knew that voice. Her eyes flew up and into the smiling eyes of the man she'd made love to the other night.

"Thanks. They're from my sister, Elle," Reid said with a nod to her.

"You? I was so worried I'd never see you again," Elle said in an excited whisper as she jumped into his arms to the surprise of her siblings.

"Me, too. But I am so glad I did. I'm afraid I may never want to let you go."

"Merry Christmas, Mr. Charles. Would you care to join us for breakfast?" her mother asked as she walked out of the kitchen with a dishtowel hanging from her shoulder.

"I would love to. Thank you. But, please call me Drake," he said, never taking his blue eyes off Elle's.

Elle thought her heart would explode. It was her mystery man. *He* was Drake Charles, *the* Drake Charles.

"I'm Reid. It's nice to meet you, Drake. Mom's told us a lot about you," he said with a grin.

"I've heard about you all, too. It's nice to meet you in person," Drake said as he shook Reid's hand. "Elle told me about y'all the other night."

"You've been dating Drake Charles and haven't told us?" Allegra asked in shock. "Oh." She cringed. "Sorry, I'm her youngest sister, Allegra."

"Nice to meet you, too."

"And I'm Bree. Sorry, we're all just a little surprised. We didn't know Elle was dating anyone, let alone you."

"It's been a whirlwind romance," Drake said with a smile. Oh, he looked even more amazing in jeans. How was that possible?

"How did you know where I was?"

"Santa told me," he said with a wink at her mother. All heads turned and looked at a very innocent-looking Margaret.

"What? I always told you I worked with Santa Claus.

It's about time you started to believe me. Come on, y'all. Help me get breakfast on the table."

Her mother turned and headed the short distance to the kitchen with her brother and sisters slowly following as they all kept looking back and forth between her and Drake.

Drake handed Elle a rectangular red box decorated with an elaborate white bow. "I have a Christmas gift I wanted to give you."

Elle held out her hands and smiled up at him. He was real and he was right here. He didn't even run when he found out it was her. He didn't mind that she was such a public figure and had to spend a lot of time running her company. Instead he found out where she was and brought her a present. So it really was everything she had thought. And more.

He took a seat on the couch next to her and brushed a kiss to her cheek. "Merry Christmas. Go on, open it."

Elle pushed off the bow. She lifted the lid to the box and looked inside. Sitting propped up among the red tissue paper was a beautiful ivory-white mask. It was simple in its style, but on the side was a cluster of small ribbon roses and a few feathers. In front of the mask sat an open velvet box with a necklace shining up at her.

Elle started to tremble as she sat quietly looking at the golden harp necklace with a diamond set at the top of the harp. Drake moved quietly and took the necklace out of the box. Taking her hands in his, he sat in front of her.

"We may have only met the other night, but that was enough to know that I have fallen in love with you. In such a short time you've already found a place in my heart. I hope the Christmas gift is okay," he said a little unsurely after confessing his feelings.

Elle wanted to speak, but she couldn't. Tears rolled

down her cheeks as she looked at the man in front of her. He was everything she had wished for and he loved her. She nodded her head and swallowed hard, finally managing to say, "Oh, Drake. This is the most wonderful Christmas gift I've ever received." Elle looked up at him; they were beginning something special.

Drake slipped the necklace around her neck and fastened it. He wrapped his arms around her tightly. "I love you, Elle," he whispered reverently to her.

"Oh, Drake. I love you, too."

Drake kissed her cheek and then the tip of her nose before placing his lips on hers. She ran her fingers through his hair and he pulled her tight against him. He had never been happier than when he knew with a certainty he would find the owner of the phone.

It had been almost eleven last night when he'd finally hacked Elle's phone and had found her mother's number, confirming it was Elle he had been with. He'd called and told Mrs. Simpson what had happened. It had been her mother who'd suggested surprising her the next morning.

He'd hung up the phone and had found his mother standing behind him with a huge smile on her face. "You've found love after all these years, haven't you?" No matter the size of the house, a mother always knows when something is up. Drake had just smiled and his mother pulled him down for a hug. "If you've finally found love, don't let her get away." That was when the plan had been hatched.

Drake had called the father of one of the children at the hospital and had asked for a favor. Drake had met him at his downtown jewelry shop just after midnight and stared in amazement at the harp. Her nickname fit her and he had been drawn to her father's story as if it were his own. He had known that night that he'd go through hell to find her again, just as the myth of Lyra had told. Drake had also brought a few presents for the man's kids in appreciation for his cooperation so early on Christmas morning. In just under an hour, Drake had been armed with a necklace, waiting until morning.

As he'd hurried to his car that morning, his parents had raced after him. "We'll stay in the car until you come get us. But we have to meet the woman who stole my Huggy Bear's heart," his mother had shouted. So Drake had let them come and ended up telling them all about Elle as he'd driven to Mrs. Simpson's house.

The kiss he had begun moments ago quickly heated up before he was hit in the head with a pair of fuzzy dice. Looking up, he saw her brother smiling and her mother and sisters hugging each other with tears in their eyes. Drake laughed but didn't move from where he held her close. "My parents . . . I forgot. They're waiting out in the car."

"You left your parents in the car?" Elle tried to scramble up, but he wouldn't let her.

"Sorry, sweetheart, you're not leaving my side yet. I'm still afraid you'll disappear again." He didn't plan to let her go far from his side for a very long time.

"I'll get them," Margaret said as she dried her tears. "Oh, congratulations, you two. My husband and I couldn't have picked anyone better to love our Elle." Drake stood with Elle and hugged her mother before she hurried outside. Elle's sisters and brother similarly hugged and shook hands with Drake. The warm family welcome let him know they cared for each other very much.

"Nice bunny slippers. Very sexy," Drake said once the introductions were over. He caught her looking down in embarrassment at her bunny-clad feet. Somehow she looked even more beautiful this morning in nothing more than pajamas and slippers instead of the gown and heels from before. Her face, completely free of makeup, glowed with happiness, and her hair, slightly messed from sleep, reminded him of what he wanted to do with her in bed as soon as possible.

The front door was thrown open as Margaret and his parents hurried inside looking like the best of friends.

Elle loved his parents and felt welcomed into his family instantly. The mothers shooed everyone out of the kitchen and made breakfast while Drake and his father entertained them with stories. They encouraged her sisters and brother to tell their own as well. Allegra and Bree, who weren't normally so relaxed with new people, were delighting the group with stories of disgruntled models and construction site high jinks. Reid then had them laughing with silly cheating scandals from his casinos.

Elle sat tucked under Drake's arm with her hand on his thigh and smiled. She'd found her happily-ever-after and she couldn't wait to see what came next.

Soon the house was filled with merriment and laughter as Christmas Day celebrations continued. Off in the distance, bells were ringing and Elle thought she heard someone bellow, "Ho-Ho-Ho, Merry Christmas!"

Chapter Ten

"**D**rake and Elle, sitting in a tree. K-I-S-S . . ."

"Shut up, Allegra!" Elle laughed as she threw one of her bunny slippers from under her desk at her sister.

"I-N-G," Bree continued to sing until she caught the other bunny slipper on the face.

Elle placed her elbows on the large desk and leaned forward. "Seriously, I don't want anyone to know."

"Don't want anyone to know what?" Mallory asked as she came into the room and took a seat on the edge of Elle's desk.

"That Elle's finally getting laid," Bree said with a smile.

"By a hot sexy recluse," Allegra continued. Elle felt her face turn red as Mallory simply arched one perfectly shaped eyebrow. "Can you guess who?"

"Hmmm. Sexy recluse?" Mallory pondered and then smiled. "You're getting some from Drake Charles?"

Elle tossed her hands up and fell back against her leather office chair.

"He even gave her that necklace for Christmas last week," Allegra tattled.

"Oh, how sweet," Shirley, Elle's father's secretary, prattled as she and her walker slowly made their way into the office that was suddenly filling up. Shirley had to be a hundred if she was a day. Her walker alone was old enough to drink. Today her walker's big black horn had shining pink, purple, and silver tinsel hanging from it with a *Happy New Year* banner hung on the front between the metal bars.

When Elle's father passed away, Shirley had made it her personal mission to ensure the girls succeeded. Shirley had meant to retire but kept saying she'd do it next month. In the meantime, she had been promoted to office manager. She ran a tight ship and also knew everything going on in the office. Shirley would turn up her hearing aids and slowly walk through the offices to see who was working, who was playing solitaire, who was dating . . . and when to crash a conversation like she did now.

The multicolored crystals on her neck cord jangled as Shirley shoved her thick glasses up the bridge of her nose to get a closer look at Elle's necklace. "A harp, oh my. I daresay your father would approve." Shirley smiled.

"Thank you, Shirley. But we are really trying to keep it quiet. Family only, okay?" Elle instructed as she fingered her necklace. Drake's thoughtfulness still brought a smile to her face.

"Only family, huh? Looks like I was left out again," a plaintive voice said.

Elle looked up at her cousin Mary and felt her heart plummet. Her cousin had a sensitive streak a mile wide. Mary was just a year younger than Elle and had inherited their grandfather's golden-blond hair that had turned redder as she got older, but the similarities ended there. They may have looked somewhat alike, but their personalities were totally opposite. As Mallory pointed out, Elle refused to be weak while Mary was one walking sob story after another.

Three years ago Mary's mother, Elle's Aunt Flory, had

come to her with one such sob story. Mary had been dumped by a boyfriend who had cleaned out her bank account before disappearing. Aunt Flory had bit into the fact that Elle had more money than she could ever use and refused to let it go. Then she reminded Elle of her obligation to the rest of the family they had left behind when they made it big. Elle had refrained from rolling her eyes. It was funny she'd had the gall to even make that argument when Aunt Flory had refused to help the Simpsons through rough patches when Elle was a kid. However, Elle was similarly *her* mother's daughter, and manners had been inherited along with a strong work ethic. And now, three years later, Mary still moped around the office reminding Elle and her sisters how bad her life was.

"Hi, Mary. How are you doing today?" Allegra tried asking with her cheeriest voice.

"Not so well . . . as if you all would care as you sit and count your money. We normal people have problems, you know," Mary complained as she took the seat Bree vacated in order to stand by Allegra.

"I'm sorry, Mary. Is there anything we can do to help?" Bree asked.

"No," Mary sighed. "I'm suffering from a broken heart."

"Humph," Shirley snorted. "You're wasting your time on that one. Trouble, I tell you, is Dean's middle name."

Mary's eyes went wide. "How did you know?"

"I heard you blubbering to your mother about it just this morning. You need to work more and talk to your mother less."

Mary's face went red. "You old coot! You need to turn your hearing aids down. It's none of your beeswax. Elle, fire her at once."

"Mary, I'm not going to fire her." Elle tried to hide the suffering in her voice. "Instead, I'm going to agree with her. Be careful with Dean. I don't know if he'd treat you the way you deserve."

"As if you're care. It sounds as if you have all the luck. First that hunk Chord, then the dreamy Noah, and now another Mr. Perfect."

Bree narrowed her eyes and stepped forward. "You have no idea what you're talking about Mary. Those men were horrible to Elle. Now she's finally found someone who seems to care about her. But don't you think we're all wondering if Drake Charles is just like the others?" Catching herself on the slip-up, she turned to her big sister. "Sorry, Elle. And Mary, we do care about you. No matter how many times we tell you, you just don't seem to believe us."

"Drake Charles. *The* Drake Charles. I give up. Life is so unfair."

"It looks like I have all the luck to be in a room of such beautiful women," Dean grinned as he sauntered into the office with his overly gelled hair and manicured nails. "Nothing like being the fox in the henhouse."

"Yes, but these hens will peck the fox's eyes out if he tries anything," Bree said as she crossed her arms over her chest while Mary blushed ten shades of red.

"Feisty. I like it."

Bree cringed. "I'm outta here."

"I'll join you," Shirley and Allegra said a little too eagerly as they hurried after Bree.

Elle and Mallory exchanged a look of silent laughter as Mary stared at Dean with hearts in her eyes. "So, what do you need Dean?" Elle asked.

Dean looked at Mary and winked. "Sorry, this is

confidential, babe."

Mary fluttered and with a dreamy smile got up. "Whatever you say, Dean."

"I'll walk you out, Mary," Mallory said, barely able to hide the laughter in her voice.

"I think you'll want to stay," Dean said, stopping Mallory from leaving.

Mallory shrugged and closed the door after Mary sulked out.

"Elle, it's always a pleasure to see you. I hate to bring bad news to such a beautiful woman." Dean shot her a smile she was sure he practiced in the mirror.

"What is it, Dean?" Elle asked, trying not to lose her patience. Dean was a goober, but he was one of her best salesmen.

"It's Hailey, our sales girl."

"Woman," Elle said automatically correcting him.

"That's for sure." Dean laughed before clearing his throat and turning serious. "Well, Hailey was out with Blue Diamond Financial Services last night and made a pass at Mr. Diamond."

Elle felt like banging her head on her desk. She fought daily to avoid the stereotypes of women in the workplace and now one of her employees just hit on one of the men she wanted to do business with. She could kill Hailey for jeopardizing her company's reputation.

"Thank you, Dean. I'm sorry you had to deal with an upset Mr. Diamond," Elle said before paging her secretary to bring Hailey to her office.

Dean chuckled. "Oh, Mr. Diamond wasn't upset. He loved it. It was Mrs. Diamond who had the problem. She apparently wasn't too thrilled to find Hailey's hand under the tablecloth and around her husband's . . ."

Elle cringed. "I get it. Anything else I need to know?"

"It wasn't the first time. Mr. Chevski called to renew our agreement for another year and mentioned how lovely it would be if Hailey brought him the papers. I know men and I know the tone he used. She bonked him good."

"*Dean*," Elle groaned. "Do I need to fire you, too?"

"Oh, I mean . . . well, she . . . yeah, you know what I mean. I'm just going to go. Here's the complaint Mrs. Diamond filed." Dean got up and shot her another smile along with a wink to Mallory.

The buzzer rang and Jessica notified her that Hailey was waiting. All she had wanted was a quiet day at the office. Sure, she was the CEO, but she thought of this company as if everyone in it were part of her family. But that also meant she felt more betrayed by Hailey's actions.

"Hi, Ms. Simpson," Hailey said hesitantly. She was the same height as Elle and beautiful with chestnut hair. Her full breasts were encased in a form-fitting suit. Hailey shook her hand before they both took their seats.

"Hailey, I have a complaint here from Mrs. Diamond. I'm not going to draw this out. This is unacceptable. Not only does it reflect poorly on you, it reflects poorly on this company. You only degrade yourself and all women trying to make their way in business with this behavior. I'm sorry, but you're fired," Elle said sternly as Mallory leaned quietly against the wall behind Hailey.

Hailey shot to her feet, her smooth skin red with anger. "Do you know how much business I've gotten you? I'll sue if you fire me. I'll smear your good name all over the media."

Mallory smiled tightly. "I don't think you'll be doing that. If you recall, when you were employed you signed a very specific employment contract along with a confidentiality agreement. You just screwed yourself here. You take any action against us, and I'll be the one coming after you. And I'll find every skeleton in your closet while the legal team wipes the courthouse floor with you. Now, my men will take you to clean out your desk. I trust this will be the last we hear from you."

"You'll regret this," Hailey spat at Elle before storming out of the office.

Mallory smiled sweetly, "Girls' night?"

"Sounds perfect. The day can only get better, right? I'll send a message to Allegra and Bree and meet y'all at Maggie's at seven." Elle felt the weight on her shoulders lift. She hated this part of her job, but it was made better by having her sisters and her best friend supporting her.

Drake whistled as he walked down the hall toward the computer lab. He had found himself doing that since he met Elle a little over a week ago. They had spent Christmas, New Year's, and every day in between together. He had thought himself in love after only one night together . . . and that was nothing compared to what he felt now. Every day he fell more and more in love with Elle.

"Drake!" Drake stopped walking and turned to see his assistant running toward him.

"What is it, Phillip?"

"Miss Simpson called. She said she tried your cell, but I told her you turned it off when you went to the lab."

"Did she tell you what she wanted?"

"Yes. Miss Simpson said she was sorry, but she had to cancel tonight. Something about girls' night at Maggie's and she hoped you'd understand."

"Actually, that works pretty well. The guys said they were having some problem with the new program we're working on. It looks like I'll be here late tonight anyway. Thanks, Phillip. See you tomorrow." Drake gave a single wave of his hand before placing it against the scanner and speaking into the microphone. The door opened and he stepped inside the lobby of the secure lab.

"How you doing, Jonas?" he asked the security guard as he took his phone out of his pocket and handed it to Jonas who placed it in the container with Drake's name, located behind his desk. Drake had a rule that no personal belongings were allowed in the lab. His employees were loyal, but he didn't want to tempt them to take a picture to post on social media or worse, steal any of the material they were working on.

"I'm well, Mr. Charles. Thank you. You going to be long today?"

"Probably."

"Then I'll see you tomorrow. Ray will be here in an hour to take over the night shift."

"Sounds good. Have a good night, Jonas," Drake said before entering the secure lab.

Five heads popped up from behind computers, and Drake saw the strain on their faces. They had landed a top-secret contract with the government to develop a program and subsequent smartphone application to trace IP addresses through an IP generator to the actual address of origin within minutes. Subsequently, in order to challenge the new software, Drake and his team had developed a new way to make IP addresses impossible to trace.

"What's the problem?" Drake asked as he stood behind his team looking at the monitors.

"We seem to be stuck. We've mastered the IP generator.

However, we can't beat it. Our own application won't work against it. Wouldn't that make the program flawed? We've tried everything we can think of and it seems we've only done more harm than good," Gregg, the senior technician, told him.

Drake ran his hand over his face. "So, while we are trying to help the good guys, we just developed a weapon that could defeat them?"

Drake leaned back in his chair and glanced at the clock. It was almost nine-thirty. His employees had gone home hours ago and he'd been working on the programming since then. He had an idea on how to fix the problem in the system, but he needed to run it by Gregg tomorrow to get his thoughts before doing anything permanent.

"Good evening, Mr. Charles," Ray said as he reached for the container holding his cell phone.

"How are you doing, Ray?" Drake asked while he pulled his cell phone out and turned it on.

"Doing right well, thank ya." Ray smiled and Drake returned it. Ray was a good ole country boy from just outside Atlanta. His mother had gotten sick and he'd picked up this second job to help the family out. "You have a good night."

"You, too, Ray. And tell your mom she can send in cookies anytime she wants." She had baked some cookies before Christmas and people where still talking about them.

"I'll tell her, but you may be buried in them now that she knows you like them."

"Ah, but what a way to go."

Drake headed out of the lab and started reading all the text messages from Phillip about his schedule tomorrow and then the messages from Elle. He almost laughed out loud when he read them. She started this afternoon telling him she was going out with the girls at Maggie's. Then came the texts from Maggie's. He was pretty sure Elle had made the cardinal mistake of leaving her phone on the table. One of the girls must have grabbed it before it locked. *Come over here you sexy beast* just didn't sound like Elle. Making the last-minute decision to see if she was still there, he walked out of his building and started walking the three blocks to Maggie's.

Chapter Eleven

Elle set down her drink and tried to swallow as she laughed at Bree's latest story from the construction site. Her sister's no-nonsense attitude, mixed with her uncanny ability to tell dirty jokes, tended to throw the male workers off balance. Simpson Steel was in the middle of a construction job, and Bree was working with a new crew who had just caught on to her dry sense of humor.

"Oh my gosh, it's almost ten. I better get home. I have meetings in the morning with the old fogeys from the bank we took over last year. They are always so hard to deal with. I mean, can you yell at someone with bushy eyebrows who can hardly hear? But, I swear, if they call me 'little missy' one more time, I'm turning Shirley loose on them," Elle joked as she grabbed her purse.

"Sorry, sis, you always like financials. I, on the other hand, will be shopping for the fall collection. Really throw them off, wear something sexy," Allegra laughed as Elle rose and gave them all hugs.

"They'd probably have a heart attack, and I don't think that would be good for business. Thanks for the night out, ladies," Elle called as she headed out the door.

Elle's smile still lingered on her lips as she dug around in her purse for her cell phone. She had to call Drake and explain the texts from Mallory. Good thing she loved her best friend. While she loved spending time with Drake, after a day like today she needed her goofy girl time.

Umph! Elle slammed into a strong male chest and stumbled backward before she was able to catch herself. She looked up into the eyes of Chord. Perfect. Her great evening was ruined by Chord's sneering face.

"Excuse me, Chord," Elle said as nicely as she could. She would not stoop to his level and start an argument. She gave him a tight smile and walked past him before she felt his hand close just a little too tightly over her upper arm.

"All alone again, Ellie? I guess money can't buy happiness." He squeezed her arm a little more and Elle couldn't help but grimace.

"I see money can't buy manners either," Elle shot back to him as she yanked her arm from his clutch. She fought the urge to rub it but refused to allow him to see how he affected her. There was something in his sneer of menacing evil that told her he'd take pleasure in seeing her hurt.

"You know, the company I'm working for, Titan Industries, is interested in forcefully taking you over. I'm sure you already know it, though. I just want to make sure you know when they take you over, I'll be involved. I thought you'd like to know when they start looking up your skirt, so to say, that I told them I knew from personal experience they'd like what they see." Chord leered at her and Elle suppressed a shudder, knowing she'd had sex with this man. She had been fooled by him and allowed him into her heart and body. She fought back the nausea building in her stomach and stood her ground.

"Why don't you remind them what happens when someone comes after me? Eager to be unemployed again?" Elle managed to ask with enough steel to her voice that

Chord's sneer fell from his face.

There was no mistaking the anger in his eyes as he reached for her again. Elle stepped back and right into someone else—someone tall and strong from the feel of his hard chest against her back. She only hoped he wasn't with Chord. But by the way Chord's eyes narrowed at the intrusion, she had her answer.

"This is a private conversation and you're interrupting," Chord said in a tight voice.

"Really? Did you know conversations involve words and not assaults, or do you need someone to teach you some manners?" Elle felt relief flood her. She knew that voice and she was definitely safe.

"Funny, I just told him he needed to learn some manners, too," Elle said as she looked up at the man giving her support.

"Well, you know what they say about great minds." He smiled down at her.

"Who the hell do you think you are?" Chord asked angrily as he realized he was suddenly being ignored.

"I'm her boyfriend. Who are you?" Drake asked in a voice that had Elle shivering as if from frostbite.

Chord took in Drake's jeans, beat-up black leather jacket, and slightly messed hair, and smiled triumphantly. "What, you work in the mailroom or something? Have to go after the hired help now, Ellie?"

Chord didn't bother to hold out his hand. Instead he flicked his business card at Drake. "Chord McAlister of Titan Industries."

Drake grabbed the card and stuffed it in his pocket. It had taken a lot of restraint not to punch this guy as soon as he saw his hand clamped around Elle's arm. Drake had broken into a run the last block to reach her as quickly as possible. When he saw her say something that changed the man's face from taunting to anger, Drake stepped out of the shadows and behind Elle. He wanted to be there in case Chord decided to act upon that anger.

While Elle hadn't said his name, he knew all about Chord. When Elle had told him the story of the attempted takeover and how she had handled it, he had been so proud. The business world was out for blood and Elle had solidified her place in it when she had decimated the company that had come after her. That kind of story spread like wildfire, and Chord's name had been attached to it as the man who had assisted the owners in their underhanded attempt.

"Chord?" Drake contemplated. "Nope, never heard of you."

"You didn't tell him about us, Ellie?"

"Ellie? Guess you weren't with her long enough to know she hates that nickname. Wait?" Drake looked down at Elle and grinned again. "Chord, *the* dumbass that tried to take over your company and then had to leave the state after you utterly destroyed him without saying one word?"

Chord's face twisted in anger and Drake enjoyed the direct hit.

"Well, I'm back now. In fact, I was just telling my Ellie here how we're going to be spending more time together. The company I work for is interested in Simpson Global. It looks like I may be your boss soon," Chord said happily.

"Oh, I doubt that on many levels. Sorry, where are my manners? My mother will have my hide if she finds out I didn't introduce myself. I'm Elle's boyfriend, Drake Charles."

Drake watched with pleasure as recognition of his

name hit Chord. His eyes shot between Elle and Drake and then locked where Drake's hand cupped her hip in a clear sign of intimacy.

"Drake Charles? *The* Drake Charles?" Chord stuttered.

"Well, it was a pleasure meeting you, Chord. Have no worries, Elle's in much better hands now. Good night." Drake squeezed Elle's hip before placing his arm on her shoulder and tucking her against him as they turned away from Chord and walked down the street.

"Thank you," Elle whispered as she laid her head on his shoulder.

"Haven't you figured out I'd do anything for you?"

Elle stopped and looked up at him. "Then take me home and make love to me. Make that the way I end my day — with happiness and love."

She was so beautiful, inside and out. He ran the back of his finger from her cheek to her chin where he lifted her face a fraction to place a slow, deep kiss on those perfect lips. "I can definitely do that."

Elle sat back in the leather chair and crossed her legs. The old trustees of the bank she was talking to had called her *little missy* eight times, *li'l darlin'* five times, and *doll* three times. Pretty soon she was going to crack. But for now she just maintained her pleasant smile and waited for them to vent all their frustrations at the fact *li'l darlin'* was now in control of the bank they had run into the ground. For some reason, she couldn't get them to understand people's money in those banks was what should matter, not if the annual meeting was held in Atlanta instead of in Hawaii.

The soft knock at the door had her looking up as one of

the bankers droned on about how unfair it was that Elle refused to pay for the exclusive golf club membership that had previously been paid out of company funds.

Jessica popped her head in and one look at her normally unflappable assistant had Elle rapping her knuckles twice on the table. "Gentleman. I understand your concerns. But in order to bring the financials up to an acceptable level of stability, we need to make sacrifices."

"Now look here, little missy . . ."

"So, let's focus on the good news," Elle interrupted. "The banks are getting stable and growth has begun again. Our customers are happy and that's even better news. Now, I believe we've discussed the plans for this year. Please don't hesitate to call if you have any more concerns. But I have another appointment right now. Thank you for coming in."

Elle strode from the room and into her office where Jessica was waiting nervously. Elle sat behind her desk and kicked off her heels. "What is it?"

"Um, I don't know how to say this," Jessica started.

"How about with words," Elle said as nicely as possibly. She'd never seen Jessica so upset.

"Okay." She let out a breath and focused. "This morning after you started your meeting, I got a call from one of the local news stations wanting a comment on your relationship with a rival CEO. I was surprised, but I didn't say anything. I followed policy and said our standard, 'I don't have the authority to issue a statement. But I can make an appointment with someone who does' line."

"What then?" Elle asked. She didn't like where this was going.

"Well, then all the news stations called. All asking

about your relationship with this CEO. And then the national stations started calling *and* the tabloids. They were asking about the news that the CEO of Simpson Global was unmarried and pregnant after a one-night stand with a rival company's CEO."

Elle felt her mouth drop, but she couldn't find any words. She sat staring open-mouthed at Jessica as she relayed the questions.

"And now it's on the news. They are saying Simpson Global has not responded to the story. Are you okay?"

"Oh my gosh, my mom is going to hear this," Elle groaned.

"Yeah, about that," Jessica held up a handful of messages. "She already has."

Elle dropped her head to her desk and closed her eyes. This was not good.

"Are you okay?"

"Don't worry, Jessica. I'm not pregnant."

"Are you even dating anyone?"

"Yes, I'm dating Drake Charles. We had been trying to keep it quiet. Crap. I need to call him, too." Elle raised her head from her desk and into Jessica's surprised eyes. "Okay. Get the emergency ice cream from the kitchen. I have some calls to make."

"Rocky Road or chocolate brownie?"

"I think Rocky Road is appropriate. And thank you, Jessica. Continue doing exactly as you are. I don't need to put out a press release just because I'm dating someone. And I certainly don't want to stoop to the level of the pregnancy question."

"Is he nice?" Jessica asked quietly as she prepared to leave.

"He's wonderful." Elle smiled.

"Then screw them. I'm happy for you, Miss Simpson."

"Thank you, Jessica."

Elle picked up her phone and called Drake first. "Hey, I heard the good news. So, when am I going to be a father?" Drake laughed.

"I'm so sorry. It had to be Chord."

"I figured that. Don't worry about it, sweetheart. It was bound to come out sooner or later. I'm just surprised it's 'rival CEO' and not my name. Kind of strange since we're not even rivals. By the way, my parents are thrilled. They can't wait to become grandparents," he laughed again.

Elle looked up as Jessica came into the office with a pint of ice cream and a spoon. She saw the spoon in Jessica's mouth and knew it was a pint apiece kind of day as Jessica set the ice cream down before hurrying to her desk to the answer the ringing phone.

"Oh no, I still have to call my mother," Elle groaned and then took a bite of ice cream.

"We'll talk baby names over dinner."

"Drake!"

"Fine, I guess we'll crush my parents' hearts. No, really, Elle, it'll pass. You know a little press isn't going to scare me away. I love you."

"I love you, too, but I can't do dinner tonight. I have a dinner meeting with a company we've been interested in for over a year. I've been trying to get them to join Simpson Global, and they have finally agreed to sell. But now I need to go call my mother," Elle sighed.

"Good luck. I'll call you tonight."

Drake hung up the phone and rolled his eyes as Phillip tried to play off being caught eavesdropping. "Come on in, Phillip."

"So no bun in the oven?"

"Not yet."

"Whoa! Yet?"

"Yet. If it were up to me I'd already be married to her, but Elle hasn't had the best relationships and I want to spoil her for a while. Show her what it's like to be won over. By the way, I met her ex last night."

"Is he better than you?"

Drake raised an eyebrow as his best friend took a seat and stretched his legs out.

"What? You know every guy asks that when they meet an ex."

"Her ex is Chord McAlister."

"Definitely better than him."

"I interrupted a conversation they were having. His hand was around her arm so tightly she had bruises this morning. Here's his card. Find out everything you can."

"You want me to . . ."

"No. I'll take care of this one personally. I know she's strong enough to handle her own battles. Look at what she did to him before. But no one hurts the woman I love."

"Look at you getting all chivalrous. I'm outta here before you start extolling the color of her eyes and the feel of her skin."

"Thanks, Phillip. Let me know if anyone finds out it's me she's dating. I'll talk to Elle tomorrow about how we should handle it if the story doesn't die down before then."

"Will do."

Drake pulled up the news and let out a long breath. He opened the top drawer of his desk and pulled out the black box. Opening it, he looked down at the ring he was planning to give Elle. Dammit. If he did it now, she'd think it was just to protect her from this news. He put the ring back and closed the drawer. He was just going to have to bide his time for the perfect moment.

Chapter Twelve

Elle walked into the restaurant with her head held high. If she could handle her mother, then she could handle this deal. She was led past the white linen-covered tables to a private room in the back of the exclusive restaurant. Mr. Tompkins was waiting for her and stood when she entered.

"Mr. Tompkins, it's nice to see you again," Elle said as she held out her hand. The man, a good thirty years her senior with graying hair, shook it before sitting down after her.

"Thank you, Miss Simpson. You, too." Elle glanced down at the glass of wine in front of Mr. Tompkins and the iced tea placed in front of her. She narrowed her eyes and gazed at Mr. Tompkins as he tried very hard to study the menu.

Elle raised her hand and waved the waiter in. "I'll have a glass of wine as well. Whatever he has is good. Thank you."

The gray head that had been buried in the menu popped up. "Wine? Do you really think that's a good idea in your condition?"

"If by condition you mean having to spend the day telling your mother you're not pregnant and trying to figure out where such a report came from, then yes, I do think it's a good idea."

"Well, it does bring up a point that I'm worried about. I wanted my company to join Simpson Global because of its stability. But hearing reports on the news about your liaisons with a rival and apparent fake pregnancy doesn't lead me to have much faith in this merger."

The glass of wine was placed on the table and the waiter hurriedly left the room, obviously feeling the tension between Elle and Mr. Tompkins.

"I mean," Mr. Tompkins started when the door shut, "if you're too busy dating, then how can I trust you to properly run the company?"

"Mr. Tompkins, how's your wife, Gloria?" Elle asked with all politeness.

Mr. Tompkins stared for a second and then gentlemanly manners took over as he went with the change of subject. "She's well, thank you. Our daughter is about to get married, so she's up to her eyes with planning."

"Congratulations. A wedding is always such a blessing. What does your daughter do?"

"She's runs her own boutique on Peachtree. She makes the most beautiful clothes," he said with fatherly pride.

"Really? You should have her call my sister, Allegra. She's the vice president of our fashion house. How wonderful she runs her own business. And if I recall, you've been in charge of your company for what, thirty years? It must run in the family," Elle smiled sweetly.

"Close. Thirty-six years."

"Time flies, doesn't it?" Elle smiled while Mr. Tompkins bobbed his head. "Now, when did you marry Gloria?" she asked conversationally.

"We've been married thirty years next month if you can believe it." The man smiled with obvious love for his wife.

Elle beamed at him. "That's great. I hope to have a love like that someday. Did you date Gloria before you started running your company?"

"No, I met her three years after I took over the company. We met on a blind date."

"Oh, how sweet. How did your daughter meet her fiancé?" Elle asked as she took a sip of her wine.

"He came into the store looking for a gift for his sister. They hit it off right away. He's a great guy. Works in production in the weather studio. He runs the national weather programming."

"Amazing," Elle said as if she'd never heard such a thing before. Her tone obviously out of character with the conversation.

Mr. Tompkins looked at her in confusion. "I'm sorry, what's amazing?"

"That while running a company you were able to date, marry, and have a child, all while your company continued to grow. Then that child even went on to start her own business, date, and now marry, while I presume still growing her boutique." Elle's smile grew cold. The seriousness on her face showed that she wasn't willing to let the hypocrisy go unchecked.

Mr. Tompkins stopped with his wine glass in midair, his eyes widening at her cold look and tone. He swallowed loudly and put the wine glass down.

"You see, Mr. Tompkins, I don't take too kindly to double standards. Now if you asked if I was really dating a rival, then I would tell you, 'No, I'm not.' Instead, you attack my ability to run a company while I date. Even though you did it and your daughter did it. Why do you think I can't? Furthermore, I think we need to get one thing straight here. I think your company is wonderful, but I'll still be a global powerhouse without it . . . what will you be if *I* decide not to bring your company into my family?" Elle sat back in her chair and stared him down.

Mr. Tompkins face went from white to pink with embarrassment in a split second. "I'm so sorry, Miss Simpson. I didn't mean to imply . . ."

"Yes, you did."

Mr. Tompkins let out a long breath. "You're right. I did. I just blew this, didn't I?"

"Yes. But my mother taught me not to throw the baby out with the bath water. I won't hold your employees accountable for your mistake. However, I am changing my offering price to this." Elle wrote a figure on the low end of the fair market value when she had been prepared to offer on the high end, and slid the paper across the table. It was still a fair offer, but one to show him she wasn't to be pushed around. "Take it or leave it, Mr. Tompkins. I'll give you five minutes to think it over."

"I don't need five minutes. You're right. This is about my employees. I know you'll take good care of them. I'll take it."

Elle stood and held out her hand. Mr. Tompkins similarly stood and shook on the deal. Elle allowed her face to soften and smiled brilliantly at him. "Thank you so much. Welcome to the Simpson family."

"Thank you for not holding my gaffe against my employees," Mr. Tompkins said with the relief clear in his voice. "And I'm truly sorry."

"I know you are. It's why I didn't walk out a minute ago."

"Um, are you really dating a rival?" he asked hesitantly.

"No, I'm dating Drake Charles. Good night, Mr.

Tompkins, and please give my congratulations to your wife and daughter."

Elle stood and left Mr. Tompkins sitting wide-eyed as she walked out of the restaurant. Her celebratory strut was cut short when she opened the door and was met with flashbulbs.

"Miss Simpson! Who are you dating?" the reporters called out.

"Is it true you're pregnant?"

"Is Simpson Global stable or is this a play by someone to take over the company?"

"Should you be drinking wine when you're pregnant?"

"Why did you email us if you didn't want to comment?"

The reporters shouted as they pressed in on her. The lights blinded her as she lost her way in the crowd. But then strong arms encircled her and pushed the reporters back, allowing her to regain her bearings.

"Finn," Elle said quietly with relief as she took a deep breath before turning to face the crowd. "Ladies and gentlemen, I will remember which of you were here and you will not be allowed in any of my press conferences with behavior like this. That includes the one I'm holding tomorrow morning," Elle lectured in her best imitation of her mother. Some of the reporters immediately backed off while others pressed forward.

Finn opened the door and Elle gracefully got in before the reporters could start firing off more questions. She'd never been left speechless before, but she'd been so surprised. They'd been so aggressive that she had no idea how to respond. Elle groaned at the thought of how she was going to look on the news tonight.

"You all right, Miss Simpson? They didn't hurt you, did they?" Finn asked as he drove away as fast as he could.

Elle felt her head swimming, but she kept her chin up and looked straight ahead as the cameras continued to film. She wouldn't let them see the turmoil inside her. The pain and worry that was knotting her stomach was not only for her, but also for her company, her family, and her employees. No, they would never see her upset.

"Thank you, Finn. You're a lifesaver."

"What was that all about?"

"I don't know. They think I emailed them a press release saying I was pregnant by a rival CEO. Why they think I would send that out, I have no idea."

"I get it," Finn nodded knowingly as he drove her out of downtown.

"Would you care to share, because I don't." Elle closed her eyes. She still felt the reporters closing in on her and took deep breaths to calm herself.

"Mind games. Happened all the time when I was playing ball. You say something to throw the opposing players off their game. Start a rumor their favorite coach was leaving, the wife of the pitcher is having an affair . . ."

"That's horrible!"

"Doesn't mean it doesn't happen. So, let me ask you this. Do you have any competitors who would want to mess with your game?"

Elle grinned with sadness and exhaustion as she reached for her phone to call her public relations team. "They all would."

Drake almost fell off the treadmill when the image of Elle being hounded by reporters appeared on the nightly news. They reported that, even though they received a press release from Simpson Global about the pregnancy, Miss Simpson was neither confirming nor denying the report. The reporter's image hadn't even faded from the screen when his phone rang.

"She's not pregnant," Drake said as a way of answering his mother's phone call.

"Didn't you listen to the interview? They said it was emailed from her office. Now maybe someone slipped and sent it before it was time, but why would she have a press release if she wasn't pregnant? Do you know when she's due? She must have just found out. Oh, I'm so excited!" His mother rambled as she completely ignored Drake's attempts to interrupt her.

"Mom! She's not pregnant. I gotta go. Love you." Drake jumped off the treadmill and wiped his face and bare chest with a towel before hurrying down the hall toward his office.

His mom had just said something that stuck out. It was a simple fact. Elle would never have approved a press release like this, which meant someone else had. The only question was who.

Drake dialed his phone and waited for Elle to answer. Her eyes had gone wide when those reporters had pushed in on her. It was the first time he'd seen her nervous. But then Finn had come and, with a firm touch to her arm, had brought his Elle back. She had instantly straightened herself and, with all the power of a woman who ran a billion-dollar company, had lectured the reporters for their bad manners. He was so proud of her, but also very worried.

"I take it you saw," Elle answered with a sigh.

"I did. How are you doing, sweetheart? You want me to do anything? I know the person who owns one of those stations," Drake said as he turned on his computer.

"That's all right. I can take care of myself. I was actually doing that when you called. Mary and I are drafting a statement for a press conference tomorrow morning," Elle told him.

"Actually, I wanted to ask you something. What's this email they keep talking about?"

"I don't know. Finn thinks it's a competitor playing mind games. He thinks they're trying to distract me from my work so they can beat me at some deal or something."

"He has a good point. I was thinking the same thing."

"Whoever it is, I'm going to destroy them as soon as I find them. If the business industry thought what I did to Chord and his company was tough, wait until this. No one lies about me and then suggests that the company is unstable. I'm responsible for thousands of employees, and I won't let anyone hurt my family."

"That's my girl. Call me if you need anything. If not, I'll be eagerly tuned in tomorrow and won't be able to wait to hear about it over dinner."

"Thanks for the support, Drake."

His heart clinched as he heard the energy drain from her sweet voice. "You don't need my support; you're a force of nature all by yourself. But I'm happy to be here anytime you need me."

As soon as he hung up, his fingers started to fly across the keyboard. Within minutes he was looking at the press release he found in one of the reporter's inbox. With a few more clicks, he sat staring at an IP address that confirmed what the reporters had been saying—the press release had, in fact, come from Simpson Global. Worse, it had come from Elle's personal email.

Chapter Thirteen

The coffee in Elle's hand wasn't strong enough to get her through the morning. She had to once again convince her mother that the pregnancy story was false. Even her brother, Reid, had called from Europe asking if he needed to fly home and beat the crap out of Drake for getting her pregnant and not standing by her through this media circus.

Then she'd gotten mad. Not at her brother exactly, but everyone. She cared for the people of Simpson Global as if they were all part of her family. And now her own family along with her work family believed these reports enough to call and ask her why she didn't tell them she was pregnant. All those nights spent alone, then finding happiness and love after all this time with Drake. All those special memories were suddenly being turned ugly and being used to smear the good name she'd spent a lifetime building.

"Shut up, Allegra." Elle heard her sisters arguing in her office from down the hall.

"Just because you're older does not allow you to discount my ideas, Bree." Oh gosh, it wasn't even six-thirty in the morning and already her sisters were arguing.

"Both of you need to relax and leave this to me," Mallory's voice, tight with anger, floated out Elle's open office door. Elle was supposed to be meeting Mary, but it looked like saving her reputation, along with Simpson Global's, would be a group effort.

"Girls!" Shirley's voice rose above the bickering. "Don't make me call your mother. Y'all are here to help your sister, not fight."

"Just tell me who I need to knock some sense into. Last night was over the line." Elle stopped dead in her heels at the sound of Finn's deep voice.

She should have felt annoyed since she needed to work on a statement instead of walking into a room full of fighting, but they were fighting because of her — for her — with her. Knowing her friends and family were supporting her, she felt a peace surround her as she headed into her office.

"I see I'm late for a meeting I didn't know I was having." Elle smiled, suddenly a little more relaxed.

"We're here to help." Shirley grabbed her hand and gave it a squeeze.

"Thank you all. Now, what have you come up with?" Elle asked as she took a seat behind her desk.

Shirley scooted forward on her walker. Today her walker had a sticker on it that read *Cougar Alert* across the front. "So far we've established that Allegra wants to dress you for the conference in a sexy power suit. Bree wants the whole family standing behind you. Finn and Mallory want to destroy the, excuse my French, bastards who are behind this."

The small sound of a sigh filled the room. "I see you decided you didn't need me . . . again."

"Not at all, Mary. They're just showing their support." Elle tried not to cringe as Mary's face filled with silent suffering.

"Well, well, well. Aren't I just the luckiest man in the world this morning?" Everyone turned to the tall, sharply dressed man leaning against the door with a huge grin on his face.

Mallory stepped forward and gave him a blatant once-over. "Sorry, we're not interested in what you're selling."

"That may be," he said with a sexy grin, "but I bet you'll be interested in what he's selling."

"Morning. Sorry to interrupt. I'm Drake and this is Phillip," Drake said with a tight smile to those he didn't know. "Unfortunately, I come with bad news."

"Get in line." Mallory held out her hand. "Mallory Westin, by the way. Nice to meet you, Drake." She flashed a grin that completely changed her appearance and Elle almost laughed at the way Phillip's eyes widened in appreciation.

Mary shrank into her seat as Phillip leaned against the wall near her and gave her mousy cousin a wink.

"Okay, will one of you tell me what's going on?" Elle asked a little nervously. Neither Drake nor Mallory looked pleased. In fact, they looked to be in pain.

"Ladies first," Drake said chivalrously.

"I knew I liked you," Mallory tossed over her shoulder before taking out a piece of paper and handing it to Elle who read it and then handed it to Drake. "Hailey's back. She commented on every news article online and on social media. She bashed you six ways to Sunday and twice on Tuesday for good measure."

"Who's this woman? And why does she obviously not like you?" Drake asked as Phillip looked over Mary's shoulder to read the paper.

"I fired Hailey last month. She was trading sexual favors for sales. She thought she was doing me a favor and wasn't happy that I fired her. Mallory had to threaten her with a lawsuit to remind her of the confidentiality agreement she signed with us. Apparently she's deciding to ignore that agreement. Bree, can you notify the legal department?"

"On my way," Bree said as she pulled out her cell phone and headed into the hall to wake the legal team.

"There's more," Drake said with a grim look. "I traced the IP address of the email sent to the reporters. It originated from Simpson Global. Not just that, but it came from Elle's email address."

"What does that mean?" Mary asked shyly from her seat.

"It means," Drake started seriously, "that the person who sent the press release did so from your network and from Elle's account. They could have sent it from any computer in the building or even from the sidewalk if they managed to hack your Wi-Fi password and Elle's account."

"Mallory." Elle didn't need to say anything else. Her friend was already heading for the doors. She'd be setting her best computer people on the email Drake would forward to them.

Elle felt all the confidence in clearing her name start to plummet. The worried looks on everyone's face said the same thing. Everything pointed right at Simpson Global and specifically at Elle. How could she clear her name when the reporters had been right? She had issued that press release.

"If you don't mind, it's time to get my sister ready," Allegra said with as much pep as she could. As the baby of the family, everyone spoiled her. Luckily, Allegra took that spoiling and became the happiest, most optimistic child Elle had ever known. At a time like this, she sure needed to borrow some of that optimism from her sister.

"Sure, dear." Shirley started to shuffle from the room and stopped by Phillip. "I'll let this fella help me out into the hall."

"Grrrr," Phillip growled with a wink as he took in Shirley's cougar sticker. He walked her out behind Finn and a very reluctant Mary.

Drake leaned over the desk and kissed her lips softly. If only Elle could escape with him. What had felt so right, so perfect, suddenly felt uncomfortable. She was worried a photographer would jump out at them and accuse Drake of knocking her up in an attempt to take over Simpson Global.

"I'll stand with you during the press conference if you choose. I'll be right out here if you need anything."

"Thanks." Elle fell back in her chair and felt the weight of fear pushing her down.

"Come on, sis. I'll have you looking so hot, the reporters will be tongue-tied." Allegra unzipped a black garment bag and pulled out an elegant suit. It screamed power but was cut to emphasis Elle's femininity. It was simply beautiful.

"Allegra, this is perfect. Thank you."

Her sister blushed. "Thanks. It's one of my own designs. Kristoff at Elegance made it for me," Allegra explained. Kristoff had been one of the first up-and-coming designers Allegra had brought into their company.

"Okay, do your damage, Allegra," Elle tried to tease as she slipped on the dark blue suit her sister had created.

Drake stood behind the partially closed door in the room attached to where Elle was giving her press conference. He watched Elle read from her prepared statement on a small television as his gut tied itself into knots.

By the time Elle had emerged from her office with Allegra, she looked like an avenging angel in a suit. She had walked onto the podium with complete confidence and demanded respect with her polite, yet firm, authoritative voice. She'd even smiled at the cameras before starting her speech. But Drake felt her fear. He felt the insecurity she hid and it bothered him more than anything to know he was standing here unable to fix it.

Women had come and gone from his life over the years. He had never formed attachments. He'd always been too paranoid to believe a woman would want him for him alone. And usually he'd been right. But the night he met Elle, his world had changed. Where there had been routine, there was now excitement. Where there had been doubt, there was now hope. He loved this woman and he would do anything to protect her — even walking into a roomful of reporters and coming out of his self-imposed public exile.

"Let me assure the public, the shareholders, and all the employees of Simpson Global that the company is not only stable, but it is thriving. We just added over two hundred new jobs this month here in the state of Georgia and look forward to adding more," Drake heard Elle say through the door. On the screen he saw a reporter raise his hand and Elle nod her head at him.

"Then how do you respond to the allegation that you're pregnant by a competitor? You say your private life is private, but wouldn't that risk the stability of the company if you were . . . um . . . close with a rival?"

Drake swallowed hard and buttoned his suit coat with trembling hands. It was time to step back into the spotlight. He strode to the door and opened it. No one looked at him until he stopped to stand next to Elle on stage. From behind the podium, she slipped her hand into his and held on tight.

He had to give her credit; she didn't show the surprise of seeing him on her face.

"As I've said, we believe these reports are being made by a competitor to damage Simpson Global's reputation," Elle repeated.

"Who's that?" a reporter asked as everyone else nodded with their pens poised to write down this sudden revelation.

"I told you I want my private life private, but due to a competitor's insecurities and unethical tactics, I unfortunately must bring my private life to light. I will only address this once and will not answer any questions on the matter after this point. This . . ." Drake looked down at Elle as she paused and smiled at him. Her hand trembled in his and at that moment being foisted back into the spotlight was worth it if he could help the woman he loved. ". . . is the man I'm dating."

"What's your name?" a reporter called out.

"You forgot me so soon?" Drake teased as he slipped surprisingly easily back into his public persona. He put a hand to his heart. "I'm wounded."

Drake smiled down at Elle as the reporters started whispering to one another. He felt her hand relax in his as the tone of the press conference shifted.

"Aren't you going to tell us your name?" a young reporter asked. Drake smiled at her and shook his head. Sure, all those years ago he looked completely different with long hair and lanky limbs. Add to it the fact that most of the reporters were younger so they probably had no idea who he was. Therefore he decided to distract them from Elle and have some fun with them at the same time.

"It's like a dagger to the heart. I can't believe you all have forgotten me. At least you won't, will you, dear?"

Drake laughed as he put an arm around Elle who laughed at him.

"I'll try not to, but only if you promise not to torture these kind people." Drake smiled wider as the reporters cheered their approval. She'd won their favor.

"Fine. Because Elle went to bat for you all, I'll give you a hint. Ready?" The reporters readied their pens. "Smartphone."

Elle just smiled and shook her head. Drake realized they were having a good time. Together they were an unbeatable team and no matter what happened at work they had won because they had each other. But that still didn't mean he was willing to overlook those who wished to harm her or their relationship.

"Drake Charles? You're *the* Drake Charles?" an older man said in shock from the back. Suddenly the room quieted down as pens scribbled, keys tapped, and tape recorders were held out.

"Ding ding ding, we have a winner! George, from Peachtree Tech Online, right?" Drake asked as the man's eyes widened in surprise. He was one of the few reporters who hadn't asked Drake about his sister. He was more interested in the business of new technologies. He was also one of the few reporters in the room Drake actually recognized. He was getting older and they were getting younger. Some of them might not even remember what a payphone was.

"Right. I can't believe you remember."

"As a prize you get three exclusive questions with me after we're finished. Thanks for playing, y'all. Until next time." Drake waved his hand to the reporters before linking his fingers with Elle and heading into the back room he'd just come from.

Finn, Mallory, and Shirley were already in the room waiting for them. Bree and Allegra followed them in from where they had stood slightly off the podium, but close enough to show their support for their sister.

He felt a rush of life he hadn't felt in a long time. He wasn't a young man without control of his emotions anymore. No, he handled the reporters in the same authoritative way Elle did, just with his own style. It was a relief. He felt as if he didn't have to hide anymore.

Elle stopped him, pulling him from his thoughts, and threw herself in his arms. "Thank you. I can handle negotiations, but you were perfect in there. I'm so sorry I had to ask you to come out of hiding," she said into his shirt as he stroked her hair.

"It was time for me to do it. I was so proud of you. We make a good team, sweetheart," Drake whispered into her hair.

"You sure do," Shirley said from across the room as the slight high-pitched sound of her hearing aid being cranked to the max filled the room.

Hearing a knock on the door, everyone turned and watched Mary walk in with George right behind her. The older man with the potbelly and too many pens in his breast pocket held out his hand to Drake. "It's good to see you again, boy. Although I guess you're not a boy anymore, are you? You know, I remember the first time I met you. What were you, maybe twenty and you had that Lamborghini. You had just bought that car when I ran into you at the donut shop over on Peachtree."

Drake shook his hand. "That's right. I think I even let you drive it around the block. George, I'd like you to meet Elle Simpson."

"Nice to meet you, ma'am."

"Elle, please. And these are my sisters, Bree and Allegra." Elle held out her hand as Bree and Allegra stepped forward to shake George's hand.

George pushed the black-rimmed glasses up his nose. "Only three questions, huh?"

"We'll start with three and then see how it goes." Elle smiled and Drake knew she'd won him over the second Jessica came running into the room with a plate of donuts. Mallory was the only one missing, so Drake guessed she'd somehow slipped out and ordered them. Mallory was a little scary that way. She seemed to know everything about everyone. Drake wasn't even surprised to find out they were George's favorites.

Elle tried not to be nervous as George took a bite of a donut and looked down at his pad of paper. He seemed like a nice enough guy, but right now she didn't know whom she could trust.

"Let's get the boring stuff out of the way. When and where did you meet?"

Next to her, Drake let out a laugh and said, "We met at a charity event last year. We hit it off right away and have been dating ever since." He answered as vaguely as possible. Elle couldn't believe the transformation from recluse to outgoing hero. At least to her he was a hero.

"Great. Now I want to hear about what you're working on," George asked as he turned his full attention to Drake as they spoke about programming and software and the next generation of smartphones.

"Last question and then I'll get out of your hair. Just to put these rumors to rest—is there any chance Simpson Global and Drake Charles Enterprises will merge?"

Elle smiled in relief at the softball he threw her. "No.

Simpson Global has no plans to merge with anyone, even DCE."

"At least not professionally," Drake winked as Elle flushed and George chuckled.

Mary quietly approached and handed George a box of donuts and offered to escort him downstairs. As soon as the door closed, Elle started to shake. The emotions of the day, the adrenaline, and the nerves all hit her as she took deep breaths.

"All this and it's only eight-fifteen in the morning." She tried to laugh as Drake quietly rubbed her back. "Let's go see what the rest of the day has in store for us."

Elle thanked Drake again and walked him to the elevator as her sisters headed to their offices. Dinner couldn't come soon enough. Just to get home into her pajamas and snuggle up on the couch with Drake would be magical. As she wiggled her toes in her uncomfortable sexy heels, she thanked the heavens she had her bunny slippers in the office. However, as Drake kissed her good-bye, her toes curled and the last thing she was thinking about were her shoes.

Chapter Fourteen

Elle looked around the hall and saw that no one was looking. She slipped off her shoes and quickly walked to her office. Someone sitting at Elle's desk clucked her disapproval, and Elle thought she'd jump out of her skin.

"Mom! You scared me to death."

"Are you really walking around the office without your shoes on? Did I raise you in a barn?" Margaret shook her head and reached down to toss Elle's bunny slippers to her.

"Thanks." Elle slipped on her fluffy slippers and fell back onto the couch.

"You did well today. And so did Drake. I don't want to be the mother who says 'I told you so,'" Margaret waved her hand in the air absently, "but you get the picture."

"Gee, so glad you could restrain yourself." Elle rolled her eyes and suddenly felt as if she were thirteen years old again. As much as she hated the I-told-you-so her mother had just *not* said, at least it showed how much she liked Drake and not the I-told-you-so she also *didn't* say after Chord broke her heart and trust.

Her mother's teasing smile faded. "How are you holding up?"

Elle blew out a breath that caused a strand of hair to float to the side of her forehead. "We'll know more at noon when this hits the local news stations and the reporters have time to write their articles, but I'm optimistic. This can't be over soon enough."

Margaret nodded. "It seems you haven't been telling me . . ."

"Elle — Mom's on her . . . Oh, hi, Mom," Bree smiled as she slid to a stop.

"Look at my daughters working together. Maybe you can work together to figure out who is playing this nasty trick on you."

Elle watched her mother stand up, smooth her slacks, and straighten her shirt with a huge smiling sun on it. She must be on her way to visit the kids at the hospital, she thought. She felt very much like a kid herself as her mother raised her eyes and gave her and Bree the same look she'd given them since they were toddlers.

"Yes, Mom," she and Bree said at the same time before giving her a kiss on the cheek.

"She still scares me," Bree said as she fell onto the couch next to Elle.

"I know." The knock at the door had both sisters letting out a sigh and looking up. "Jessica, thank goodness . . . is that double brownie chocolate chunk?"

"Two of them." Bree smiled as she thanked Jessica and took her own pint.

"Is it that bad?" Elle asked as she dug into her ice cream.

"No, that good," Jessica smiled and handed her some papers. "The reporters loved your press conference. Here are the first articles that are going up. They're eating up the love story and painting you and Mr. Charles as the new 'it' couple."

Elle let out her breath and slumped against Bree's

shoulder. Thank goodness. Now, she hoped, she could move on with her life. And if she ever saw Chord again she was going to rip off his . . . Elle took a bite of her ice cream and thought violent thoughts.

Her mother taught Elle more than the look she'd just given her daughters. She taught her how to get things done all while maintaining a polite smile. And that was exactly what she was going to do now. Smile politely and squash him like the bug he was.

"Jessica, put everything you're working on aside and call Mallory. I need the two of you to look into Chord McAlister. I need to know everything about him and the company he's working for now."

"Oh. I know that look. I almost feel bad for Chord." Bree smiled as she licked the spoon. "Now, what can I do to help destroy the bastard?"

Drake lit the candles and poured the pasta into a bowl to set on the middle of the table. Elle had been working long nights this past week since the news conference. She didn't say why, but he knew she was trying to make up any ground she lost from the fake news reports. It worked for him; he had been putting in long hours trying to solve the problem with his program for the government.

However, the news that he and Elle now were *the* most powerful couple had been nice. Not the powerful part, but the part where the papers were talking about their relationship as if it were a fairy tale. To him it was. Every day he fell more and more in love with her, even if they only saw each other for a couple hours at night. He found himself wanting to do things for her. Not because she demanded it; she never would do that. He simply wanted to show her how much he loved and supported her, so tonight he was making dinner. He'd never made a woman dinner before and felt inordinately proud of himself.

Drake tossed a salad and set it on the table. He still didn't know how he got so lucky—even if others in the media didn't see it because they were so wrapped up in what it meant. Some talked about their relationship as a power play, some as a way of getting press, and others, like the men he overheard at lunch today, were wondering who wore the pants in the relationship. But when you're in love it isn't about power. Power struggles aren't real love. It was about sharing. It was about trust and supporting each other to be the best person each can be. It was about being a team. The mind-blowing sex didn't hurt either.

The door unlocked and Drake looked up to see Elle toss her keys on the side table and hang up her coat. "It smells amazing in here. I don't know what I did to deserve this, but I'll take it." She grinned, but Drake could see the bags under her eyes. He grabbed a glass of wine and brought it to her as she kicked off her heels and shook her head at them. "Why do I have to love them so much? I mean, look at them, just lying there looking so sexy and innocent. But then you put them on, and they turn into Satan's stilettos."

"Here. Come have dinner, drink wine, and forget all about them." Drake handed her the wine and dropped a lingering kiss on her lips. He'd make sure he found a way to make her forget her shoe problems.

Elle fell into Drake's kiss. His strong arms held her to him as he slowly kissed her. A moan escaped when his hand ran down her spine to cup her bottom and give it a gentle squeeze. This week had been exhausting. Jessica had found out Chord's threat of a takeover was a little more serious that they initially thought.

Elle had wanted to ignore it, but what they found after digging further troubled her. Titan Industries had been quietly buying Simpson Global stock and had amassed a good percentage. Not enough to force her family out. When the company went public, Elle had insisted the family retain the majority of the stock, making it very difficult to be ousted. But Titan's holdings were enough to be a pain in her behind. The power players at Titan were trying to garner votes among the shareholders to replace her as CEO and she would not put up with that.

This past week, Elle had been trying to stop them from buying any more shares by talking to the shareholders. She'd also been lost in research. She was studying Chord, Titan Industries, and their CEO, Mr. Eldrich. Elle was very quietly looking for allies as she made deals to buy Titan stock in the near future. Jessica had given her a list of shareholders, and Elle had been meeting with them to set up an agreement to buy their stocks by the end of the month. She was going to have to prove herself once again as someone not to be trifled with, plus the conglomerate was very attractive. They had some very profitable holdings and Mr. Eldrich, while a respected member of the elite good ole boys club, had a reputation of being misogynistic and narcissistic. If she could sneak in the back door and take them over while they thought they were doing the same to her, it would be a wonderful investment for her company. And Mr. Eldrich's personality played in her favor. He'd never see it coming as he probably believed a woman would never be smart enough to pull it off.

"Let's eat. I have something special planned for dessert," Drake murmured against her lips as he ended their kiss.

"What is it?"

"You."

Bree slid a thick folder across the desk as she continued her report on the new construction project for Simpson Steel. Elle glanced at the permits, design plans, and orders as Bree talked about the estimated timeline of the project and financials.

Elle pulled out a piece of green paper and saw it was a letter addressed to Bree. "What's this?"

Bree's face was impassive, but she snatched the paper out of her hand. "Sorry, this shouldn't be in here. As I was saying, the architect on the project is driving me crazy."

As Bree headed back into her account of the project, Elle found her mind drifting. After her first good night's sleep, Elle felt refreshed and ready to tackle anything. She had woken up that morning in her apartment to the smell of bacon sizzling and coffee brewing. Drake made her breakfast and the two of them headed into work together. The kiss he left her with before walking down to his building was full of promise for that night.

"Earth to Elle." Bree waved her hand in front of her face as Allegra giggled.

"What?" She hadn't even realized she'd zoned out of their weekly project update meeting.

"Nothing of importance. Only a one-billion-dollar project," Bree teased as she nodded her head to Allegra. "You're up."

Allegra brought out a couple bright pink folders and handed them to her sisters. "I want to expand into the luxury market. It's a large price tag, but I talked to the owners and they hinted that Bellerose is looking for a parent company to fund expansion."

"Bellerose, aren't they the sponsors of the French Majors for tennis?" Elle asked as she put all thoughts of Drake out of her mind. This was a huge fashion house.

"That's right. They also dress many of the American and British celebrities on the red carpet. They also have huge layouts in the top fashion magazines all over the world. Their tent at last year's New York Fashion Week was packed. Now you can see why I'm so excited." Allegra was practically bouncing in her chair.

"How are they wanting to expand?" Bree asked.

"They want to expand into accessories: shoes, sunglasses, perfume, and handbags. While they're luxury and in the black financially, they need capital investment to expand that much while securing deals with high-end retailers."

"What's the price tag?"

By the time the sisters finished going over the financials of Bellerose, Elle was cross-eyed but very excited. They felt good about the purchase, and Jessica had gone to set up an initial meeting.

"Miss Simpson?"

"Yes?" All three sisters responded to Jessica as she knocked on the door and peeked in.

Jessica laughed and shook her head. "Sorry, Miss Elle Simpson, you have a visitor. It's Mr. Burger from the bank. He said he's ready with what you requested."

"Requested? I didn't request anything. Which bank is he from again?" Elle asked in confusion. Maybe he was from one of the boards?

"Peachtree," Jessica told her.

"Jess, this is Atlanta. Everything is named Peachtree. Is it First Peachtree, Peachtree City Bank, or one of the other Peachtrees?"

"First Peachtree." Jessica tried not to laugh. "The one in Peachtree Corporate Place.

"Of course, show him in." Elle shrugged her shoulders at her sisters as Jessica headed out of the office.

"Oh, and you'll meet with Bellerose next Thursday at nine at the Pink Champagne restaurant. I put it on your calendar," Jessica called out as she disappeared to retrieve Mr. Burger.

"First Peachtree isn't our usual bank. What's this about?" Bree asked.

"I don't know. We have a cash reserve there, but I certainly didn't ask him for anything." Elle smiled and stood as a jovial, wiry man practically bounded through the door.

"Miss Simpson, it's good to see you again. I know you said you'd stop by tomorrow, but I wanted to thank you for your business again and get it to you as fast as I could."

Elle automatically shook his hand but was too confused to return his smile. What was going on?

"Here's your money, ma'am. I'm glad First Peachtree can assist you in your new project." Mr. Burger lifted the metal briefcase he was carrying and handed it to her.

Elle placed it on her desk and clicked the locks open. She saw Bree and Allegra move to try to peer into the case as she opened it. Elle felt her breath lodge in her lungs. The brief case was full of cash.

"Two million in cash. Would you like to count it?" Mr. Burger asked and Elle heard both of her sisters gasp.

"Mr. Burger, I don't mean to sound obtuse, but why are

you bringing this to me?"

Mr. Burger's smile faltered and his brow crinkled. "It's just what you asked for this morning. You told me Simpson Global needed the cash in order to invest in a new project. When I asked you if you wanted to use the money in your money market account, you said you did. Remember?"

"You talked to me on the phone this morning?" Elle asked slowly as she tried to understand what was going on.

"No, you came in. You had that lovely black hat with the . . ." Mr. Burger wiggled his fingers in front of his face, ". . . thingy swooping across part of your face. I told you I needed a day to get the cash together and you told me you'd stop by tomorrow to pick it up. But I wanted to get this to you as soon as possible. I didn't know if your investment was time-sensitive. Plus, you seemed aggravated this morning that you had to wait. As soon as the cash was available, I decided to rush it over to you. Is something wrong? Am I too late?"

Elle sat down hard in her chair and closed the metal case. "Why did you think it was me this morning requesting the money?"

Mr. Burger's jaw tightened and his previous jovial smile flipped to a stern frown. "Are you telling me that wasn't you?"

"That's exactly what I'm telling you."

"Whoever it was looked a great deal like you — same hair color, same height. She knew all about your sisters, even mentioned them by name. By all appearances, she was you. She even gave me your driver's license to complete the withdrawal since she couldn't remember the account number. The picture was yours. The birth date was yours. The address was even correct." Mr. Burger shook his head and pulled out his phone. "I'm calling the bank investigator. Someone just tried to defraud us of two million dollars."

Elle worried her bottom lip as Mr. Burger talked into the phone ordering an investigation. It wasn't just fraud — there was someone out there stealing her identity. If the bank believed her, who else would? The media? The shareholders? What other damage could she do, not only to Elle but to her whole company?

Mr. Burger hung up his phone with a grim look. "I am so sorry, Miss Simpson. I can't believe this happened. I assure you, First Peachtree . . ."

Elle held up her hand to stop him. "Mr. Burger, you have done nothing wrong. In fact, if it weren't for your excellent customer service, we wouldn't have discovered the error. For now, let's take the money back and put it in a new account. No one is to get into the account without one of my sisters *and* me personally appearing together to sign for it."

"That's a wise decision, Miss Simpson. While the bank investigator is looking into this incident, I would advise you to run your credit report and check on your other accounts. We'll be in contact shortly."

He picked up the briefcase and shook Elle's hand before giving a quick nod to each of her sisters. Elle watched him head out of the office but didn't say a word until the door had closed. She looked at her sisters and they immediately surrounded her with concerned looks.

"I guess it wasn't Chord after all," Elle said casually while emotions raced through her system and her stomach plummeted.

"Elle," Allegra started hesitantly. "I know Mallory mentioned Hailey. Do you think Hailey could have done all of this? I mean, could she have gotten back in to our network and sent that email? As for the bank, she is the same build as you and with a wig . . . "

"I suppose she could have. I'm sure clients weren't the only people she was sleeping with. She could have easily gotten someone else's password and sat in the lobby while she tried to destroy me like she threatened to do the day I fired her."

"How would she have known about Drake, though?" Allegra asked.

"She didn't have to," Elle sighed. "None of the press releases gave a name. I think it was just in retaliation for scolding her for using sex to do business. A perfectly ironic payback, wouldn't you say?"

Elle's sisters each gave her a hug and a supportive smile as they left her alone in her office. She wasn't going to let anyone ruin everything she'd built. No, she'd fight this just the way she fought and defeated Chord years ago. Even though he wasn't behind the press releases, he was still trying to take over her company. She was determined to go forward with the plan she and Jessica had already formulated. Elle absently rubbed her arm where he'd grabbed her last week. No, Chord was a threat and had to be handled as well. She was surrounded by threats, and it was best to never turn your back on one.

Elle pressed the intercom on the phone. "Jessica, there's something I need you to do for me."

Chapter Fifteen

Elle landed hard on her back. The air whooshed out of her lungs and her head bounced off the blue padded mat covering the floor. She saw Jessica cringe where she sat and felt like cringing, too, if her whole body wasn't already throbbing. Mallory's long blond hair almost tickled Elle's nose as she leaned over and looked down at her.

"Fun, right?" Mallory smiled. "Thanks, Finn. Let's try it again."

Mallory extended her hand and helped Elle stand up. Jessica had called Mallory at Elle's request and somehow Finn had been recruited in Mallory's attempt to prepare Elle against one of the threats facing her. Elle had to make an example out of Chord and the company he was working for. And when she made her final move, it was going to be big. It also required her to confront him, and she wasn't going to be unprepared this time.

A small conference room table and all the chairs had been moved against the far wall an hour ago. A padded mat had been placed on the floor and her self-defense lessons had begun as soon as Finn and Mallory arrived.

"Finn, I'm impressed. If you ever need a job and I hire out bodyguards, you'd be perfect." Mallory stepped back and grinned mischievously. "And the socialites would love you."

Elle almost laughed. Finn looked so embarrassed. For a former athlete, Finn was remarkably shy about his good looks. His black hair was cut close to his head in perfect straight lines that accentuated his strong jaw and sexy brown eyes. It didn't hurt either that he could send women into fits with his body alone, but she'd never once seen him act as if he were anything other than a protective brother.

"So, where did you learn those moves?" Mallory asked as she placed Elle in front of Finn with her back to his chest.

"I earned my black belt in Kenpo when I was younger. Since it focuses on speed and balance, it helped with baseball. You know, just like how some football players take ballet to improve footwork. Except, once I started it, I really liked it and have kept up with it over the years."

"*Please* say you'll come work for me. I can feel the breeze from the fluttering fans of overwrought debutantes right now." Mallory sent him a wink and then turned her attention back to Elle. "Remember, momentum and gravity. They're free and always around when you need them."

Finn reached out and grabbed Elle from behind. His muscled arm clamped across her chest, pinning her to him. Elle took hold of Finn's arm and quickly stepped back into him, causing him to move his foot. As soon as he did, she yanked him forward, bending at the waist and dropping her shoulder at the same time. Finn was pulled forward and over her shoulder by momentum. Gravity took over as he landed on his back in front of her.

"I did it!" Elle couldn't believe she'd just sent a six-foot-plus man flying over her shoulder. "Oh, are you okay, Finn?"

"I'm fine. And that is exactly how it's done. Good job." Finn stood and wrapped her up in a bear hug. "I feel better already about you ever having to confront Chord. But, just to make me feel even better, let's practice again tomorrow."

"How about we meet here at five in the morning? We can work out and then grab some breakfast before starting work."

"With all these strange things going on, I'd feel better if you let me pick you up at your apartment on the way here. Or we could even go to my gym. You could work out with some of my friends. You might pick up a trick or two. And you'd certainly be safe," Finn offered as he slipped on his black suit jacket.

Elle thought about it for a second and then nodded. As much as she hated the feeling of being protected, she knew it made sense. She was smart enough to know when to ask for help. And she planned on doing just that tomorrow.

Elle turned to address Finn, Mallory, and Jessica. "I haven't told you all this, but this isn't just about Chord. Today someone went into First Peachtree Bank and used my identity to request two million dollars from the company account."

"Oh my," Jessica gasped. Finn's eyebrow rose in surprise and Mallory fingered the pearls at her throat contemplatively as she waited for Elle to continue.

"Luckily, the bank thought it was a time-sensitive issue and brought me the money personally. The bank now has their investigator on it and I hope to hear more tomorrow."

"Are all your other accounts safe?" Mallory asked as she pulled out her phone and started typing on it.

"Yes, at the banks at least. I handled all of that while Jessica called you here. But when I called the credit bureaus, I found that two credit cards had been applied for and approved in my name this past week. I set a freeze on my account and had Legal start the process of informing the credit card companies of fraud."

"So, while Chord poses a threat to the company and you physically, there's also a woman out there pretending to be you. Do you think she's dangerous?" Finn asked.

Elle thought about it. While she didn't appear dangerous in the same sense as Chord, it was freaking her out more than she cared to admit that there was someone out there trying to take over her life. "I don't know. My sisters and I think it's Hailey. Mal had thought the rumors to hurt the company all came from her to begin with."

"But now she may be taking it another step and trying to hurt you personally? I never did like her," Jessica said as she shook her head.

Mallory's phone vibrated and she looked down at it. "Okay, I just got a text from the bank investigator. I'll meet him tomorrow to look over the security tapes and see what he's found. I'll also take him my files. What else do you need? I know that look and you're thinking of something."

"Actually, I am. I don't know how to handle Hailey, but I do know how to handle Chord," Elle said. "Jessica has been helping me by looking into the company he works for. I'm keeping this close to the vest because I don't know whom to trust anymore. Over the past week, I've lined up sellers for a near majority of Titan's stocks under the names of some of the subsidiaries we own. When they go to make their move, I'll complete the purchases and force a takeover."

"But they will grow suspicious if they see so many different companies buying up stock," Mallory told her.

"When I have it lined up with an agreement to purchase the stock, I'm pressing the Go button all at once. But, there's some stock I do need to buy to get that remaining one percent. And it's public stock that would require a name to get it. I want it bought now because there's a chance someone else could buy it on the open market and then I'll be short of the majority. I can't buy it, but you all can."

Mallory grinned. "That's devious. That's just like when Sally Jo rigged the prom queen ballot."

"Exactly. It's where I got the idea."

"So you want us to buy stock? Why again?" Jessica wondered.

"Because you'll be buying small amounts of stock this week. You can buy anywhere from ten to a hundred shares. Do it through an online account or a broker and you'll look like someone who's just dabbling in the market. I've lined up enough shares with existing stockholders that all I need is another thousand individual shares to secure a majority."

"And then we'll put our shares up for sale on the day you need us to and Simpson Global will buy them," Finn said with a slow smile spreading across his face. "That is devious."

"It's not called a hostile takeover for nothing." Elle smiled back. "Plus you can either sell them that morning or you can keep them. I just need a majority vote of shareholders to oust the board, and if you keep your shares and vote with me, then the mission will be accomplished just the same as if you sold them to me. And if I make all my purchases next Friday, the reports I have to file with the SEC won't have time to make its way onto Chord's desk. He wouldn't have time to enact a poisoned-pill vote."

"What's that?" Jessica's nose crinkled and Elle tried not to laugh. A poisoned pill in the business world wasn't what it sounded like.

"It's a way to dilute the stock so it would be harder for me to buy. I'm lining up purchases with their major shareholders at a higher price to ensure sales. Simultaneously, I've been distracting the board from that fact by whispering in ears that Chord and his company are trying to take over Simpson Global. Knowing Chord's ego, he probably thinks the stock is rising because people want to get in before they take us over."

"I like it," Mallory grinned. "I'll make the arrangements. You say you need a thousand shares? Between myself and my company, I can easily do that."

"I can buy twenty shares," Jessica said, jumping up from her chair.

Finn nodded his head as she saw him working it through his mind. "I'll buy a hundred. I know a good bet when I see one. Then you'll easily have a majority."

"We'll have the majority," Elle reminded them. "We'll be partners."

Finn's smile slipped. "Is Chord doing the same thing with Simpson Global?"

Elle rocked back on her heels and shook her head with a sly smile growing. "He thinks he is. Except he's so conceited that he bragged to me about his plan and gave me enough time to slow their progress. Our shareholders know of the attempt, and most of them are happy with the company. Many are refusing to sell and have agreed to vote against the move. Furthermore, when I took the company public, the family kept a majority interest."

"Then why bother trying?" Jessica wondered.

"Because he thinks more about himself than he does about doing research. He probably saw our names adding up to only twenty-five percent and figured it would be easy to take us over. We've never made a big deal about us owning the majority, and the majority is split up between our individual names and different trusts."

"Well," Jessica said excitedly. "I've never been a business partner before. This is going to be fun. I feel so sneaky."

Elle laughed along with Finn and Mallory. She felt some of the weight that had been pressing down on her lift away. Slowly, she was regaining some control over her life. If she could make it through the next week, then she'd celebrate by seeing if Drake could escape for a romantic weekend.

Elle felt as if she'd hardly seen him for the past week and she was sure he felt the same way. Luckily, he wasn't complaining or trying to smother her. It was the opposite. He was supportive and knew the duties of a CEO. That was a relief to her. She knew no matter what, he'd be there for her. She just hated that she had to test their relationship with distance and stress so soon.

Drake waved to the security guard in the lobby of Elle's building as he headed toward the elevators. They knew him now and didn't make him stop to sign in. Drake felt the extra beat in his heart as he stepped onto the elevator and pushed the button for the top floor.

He missed her and tonight he wanted to celebrate. He'd figured out the trouble with the program he was working on and now it worked like a dream. The government was thrilled. Now CIA, FBI, Secret Service—all of them could trace an IP address from their cell phones. Not only that, but his app could get around IP generators to find the actual location and IP address of the computer in use. Spies could use it in foreign countries to track terrorists. The FBI could use it for kidnapping cases where the criminals sent their ransom notes electronically. This app was going to change the government's fight against crime for the better.

And the second he got off the phone with the government contact this afternoon, all he'd wanted to do was share his news with Elle.

They hadn't seen much of each other this week so he'd planned a romantic night out for them. He knew running a business was time-consuming. So was dating someone who similarly ran her own business. It limited the time they had together and he wanted to make the most of what they did have. So he'd booked a private room for dinner at her favorite restaurant, followed by tickets to a small concert performance of Vivaldi for the patrons of the philharmonic. Then he planned to take her home, strip her naked, and worship every inch of her body.

The doors to the elevator opened and the hall lights were already dimmed. Most of Simpson's employees had already gone home, including Elle's secretary. He turned the corner and stopped at the open door. Her feet, clad in bunny slippers, bounced with agitation under her desk. Her hair was spilling from her pins and her hand dug into her locks above her forehead. She leaned on her elbow reading the papers on her desk, not noticing his arrival. It gave him time to look her over. Dark circles were starting to appear under her eyes and a plate of uneaten food sat on the far side of the desk. She was nothing but an exhausted, beautiful mess.

"Elle, sweetie, I've come to take you home," Drake said quietly as to not startle her. Elle looked up and Drake had to control his desire to pick her up and carry her to the car.

"What time is it?"

"A little after eight. Come on. This can wait until the morning. Let's grab some fast food and get you home."

Drake got her coat from the closet and waited for her to gather her things. She didn't complain and she didn't protest. In fact, she was so quiet he worried she was falling asleep in the middle of trying to put her heels on. She shook her head as if to wake herself up, causing another lock of hair to fall from a pin. Finally she stood and he helped her into her coat. Drake picked up her purse and with his arm around her, he took her home.

As soon as they entered her apartment, he ordered her to eat as he got a bath ready and pulled out her favorite pajamas.

"Come on, Elle. Let's get you into bed."

"I'm sorry, I never asked how your day went," Elle said as she hid a yawn with her small hand.

"It was good. Nothing that can't wait until tomorrow," he told her as he pulled out her chair and slipped his arm around her waist. She laid her head on his shoulder and let him guide her to the bedroom. The celebration could wait. Tonight he was going to take care of the woman who filled his heart.

Chapter Sixteen

D rake rolled over and threw his arm around Elle to pull her against him. His arm landed on the cool sheets instead of the warm, curvy body of his girlfriend. With his eyes still closed to the early morning light, he felt around the bed. He opened his eyes and discovered she was gone.

With a sigh, he sat up in bed and looked around the room. It wasn't even six in the morning and there was no sign of her anywhere. He stumbled to the bathroom and saw the sticky note on the mirror. *Had to leave early. Won't be home until late. Love you, E.* He wouldn't be home tonight either. Tonight the guys were coming over to his place to watch the basketball game. But it looked like Elle forgot. Drake stepped into the shower and tried not to feel disappointed as the hot water washed over him.

The sweat rolled down Elle's back as she punched the heavy bag over and over again. When Finn said he'd take her to his gym, she pictured her gym with a high glass entranceway and fancy new machines. Not a literal hole in the wall of some old warehouse. Inside was dimly lit, with punching bags along the perimeter and square padded rings in the middle. Some men boxed, some did karate, and some looked to be practicing mixed martial arts. Instead of fancy equipment, there were some benches and free weights scattered around the room.

To say she had been hesitant when she walked in was an understatement. As her eyes adjusted to the full gym, she noticed the smiles the men cast in welcome. She recognized a couple of them from music or sports. They all chatted with Finn and smiled at Elle in her pink workout shirt. But then Tigo, the owner of the gym, made his way over to them and the men went back to their workouts.

Finn introduced her to a man who had once trained professional boxers. When Finn explained why she was here, the tough man softened and took her under his wing. He called over a few of the men she'd met and they spent hours training: how to throw an effective punch, how to grapple, how to fight in close spaces, how to disarm, and now Tigo had her working the bag.

"It takes thousands of repetitions for your muscles to remember it. You want to be able to have punched so many times that your body will automatically do it before your mind has had time to process the threat," Tigo explained from his place beside her.

Elle punched the bag again and again until her knuckles swelled and her arms felt as if they would fall off.

"Good. Now you come back tomorrow and do it again," Tigo said before walking away.

Elle collapsed onto one of the benches and let her arms dangle as she lay down.

"I'm impressed, Miss Simpson. I didn't think you had it in you to last three hours here," Finn grinned from where he stood over her.

"After all of this, I would appreciate it if you called me Elle. You're a good friend, Finn."

"Well, thank you. You're a good woman. And one

who's going to be late for work if she doesn't haul ass."

Elle groaned. "I don't know if my arms work."

"Here, put this on. It smells horrible, but it works." Finn tossed her a container she thought was face cream. It bounced off her chest as she couldn't move her arms fast enough to catch it.

"Thanks," Elle picked it up and opened it. She almost found herself flat on her back again. Horrible didn't begin to describe the smell. She just hoped she had enough perfume to cover the scent or her business meeting that morning was going to be very awkward.

Drake's eyes flew over the code of a program one of his techs had brought in. In his mind, the numbers and symbols came alive and he saw the working program play like a movie. He was lost in it when he suddenly got the feeling of being watched. A shiver ran down his spine and his hair stood on end. Slowly he raised his head. The *I've Forgotten More About Sex Than You'll Ever Know* bumper sticker across the front of a walker was his first clue to who was waiting for him. He'd been so immersed in the program that he hadn't heard the door open and the walker roll to a stop in front of him.

"Shirley," Drake said, trying to quell the embarrassment caused by allowing a woman old enough to remember the dinosaurs sneak up on him.

"Mr. Charles, I think we need to have a talk." Shirley slid her dentures around menacingly and Drake cringed. When his mother used those words it was never good. He didn't know what he did, but he knew he was in trouble.

"Of course, what can I do for you? And, please, have a

seat. Can I get you anything?"

"Tea would be lovely, thank you."

Drake buzzed Phillip. A second later Phillip strode into the room and stopped dead in his tracks, his eyes widening to a point Drake thought they might fall out. Shirley looked behind her and smiled innocently. "Hello, handsome."

Drake hid his laugh behind a cough. It was clear Shirley had somehow managed to get into the office without Phillip knowing. That feat alone would give Drake something to tease his best friend about for months.

"Could you bring us two cups of tea, please?" Drake managed to ask as he tried to control his laughter.

Phillip shook his head as if to clear it and then his famous playboy smile filled his face. "Anything for my gal Shirley."

"Oh, you whippersnapper. If I was fifty years younger . . ."

Did she just purr? Drake and Phillip both flushed red. After a wink, Phillip hurried from the room.

"So young, so stupid," Shirley laughed as she shook her head. "It's amazing you men can still survive in this world. Speaking of stupid," Shirley narrowed her eyes at him.

"Me? What did I do?" Drake didn't know why, but he knew he was about to be taken to the woodshed.

"Let me tell you a story," Shirley started, but then stopped as Phillip brought in the tea.

As he placed the cup down on the table next to Shirley, she reached out and patted his hand. "You should take care of that rash, dear. Don't want it to get worse."

Phillip's face went white and then red with embarrassment. "How did you know?"

"I heard you talking to yourself as you looked at it when I went by your desk."

Phillip's eyes flew to Drake's face. "Don't look at me like that. It's just athlete's foot. I swear."

Drake just shook his head and smiled. Phillip was never going to hear the end of this. He was going to tell this story every year at the annual convention. Phillip finally threw his hands up and stalked out the room.

"Now, you were about to tell me a story," Drake reminded her as she took a sip of her tea.

"That's right. This story starts with a woman who worked at a railroad company and a dashing young man bent on making a better life for his family."

Drake listened as Shirley told how she and Mr. Simpson met when he came to human resources to make sure all his checks were mailed straight to his wife. He had shown Shirley pictures of his children and told her about his family. Shirley had felt a pang of envy; while she and her husband had a grand love affair, they were never blessed with children.

"Five years after meeting him, he found me having lunch in a diner close to our headquarters. He wanted to buy up some railroad tracts. My husband had been a higher-up in the company and knowing we were friends gave me some tips that I passed along to Mr. Simpson.

"Gerald and I retired and moved to Florida. We were going to enjoy our golden years in style. And we did. We took cruises and fell in love all over again. But way too soon, the good Lord took him away from me. I was in a state where I knew no one, with a house that only reminded me of my Gerald, and the prospect of doing absolutely nothing for the rest of my life."

Drake saw the way her cup teetered as she placed it on the saucer. "I'm sorry for your loss, Shirley."

"Fiddle-de-dee. That was over twenty years ago now."

She tried to pass it off, so Drake let her. It hit him that he'd feel the same way if something happened to Elle, and he suddenly had the urge to call her.

"There were only a couple people at the funeral and each had said their piece and left. I sat looking at the coffin for I don't know how long," Shirley continued. "I remember sitting there wishing for something to take the pain and loneliness away. I looked up and saw a sight I'll never forget. Mr. and Mrs. Simpson strode toward me, hand in hand, with their four children following close behind.

"Reid, a junior in high school, came and stood behind me with a hand on my shoulder. Bree and Elle stood beside me, each taking a hand in theirs. Little Allegra bent down and picked up my purse and smiled at me. I looked up at Margaret standing in front of me with her hand clasped in her husband's. She looked at me and with a tone that brokered no argument said, 'We've come to take you home, Shirley.'"

Drake looked away as Shirley dabbed at her eyes. He could envision it as if he had been there.

"I looked around, stunned. They weren't my family. But they had driven all the way from Atlanta to be with me. They helped me pack up our condo and put it up for sale. A week later I was part of the family, living with them in a tiny house as the girls bunked in one small room to let me have my own space. For a while I sat as the world went on around me. But at dinner I listened to Mr. Simpson talk about the small business he wanted to grow.

"Soon he was asking my opinion and one day he dragged me to his office. It was a small room in a seedy strip mall next to a travel agency. The next day as I sat in their home, I felt restless so I went to the office and offered to help with filing. Then I started answering phones. A year later we moved to a small building two blocks over. Two years after that we moved into a single floor of the building we are in now."

"The story of Simpson Global is truly amazing. Elle told me some of this, but I appreciate you sharing more."

"Oh, it's not just the story of Simpson Global I'm here to talk about. It's the people. They're my family. When Mr. Simpson died and Elle was thrust into the position to save the company, she almost quit. She was so heartbroken over the loss of her father and so outnumbered when it came to the number of people who believed in her that I found her alone one night exhausted and crying, but no tears were able to fall. She'd cried them all out of her little body. Everyone was against her. Her own mother supported her in everything she did but told her no one would think less of her if she sold the company. Reid left for Europe the week after his father was buried. Bree and Allegra were too young to understand what had been placed at Elle's feet."

The image of Elle, broken and defeated, tore at Drake's heart. She wasn't like that. She was strong. She was independent. She was the smartest, most amazing woman he'd ever known.

"I can't see Elle defeated. I just can't. She's so strong." Suddenly an image of Elle exhausted at her desk filled his mind and he wasn't so sure anymore.

"Even strong women need help sometimes. Just like strong men sometimes need the support of a good woman," Shirley said knowingly as she kept her eyes locked with his. "But I wouldn't let this happen to the family that saved me in my darkest hour. Even as she refused my help, I stood by Elle and whispered words of encouragement while Margaret grieved, while Reid disappeared to gamble with his inheritance, and while Allegra and Bree finished college.

And I was there when that good-for-nothing Chord came around. And I was there picking up the pieces of Elle's broken heart when he betrayed her."

"That won't happen again. I'm nothing like Chord. I will never betray her," Drake said passionately. He didn't know he could respect Elle anymore than he already had, but he did. Knowing what she went through to keep the family company alive . . . it was nothing short of the bravest thing he'd ever heard.

"You won't on purpose. But you already have," Shirley said quietly.

"What?" Drake's voice was harsh with surprise. He'd never betray her.

"Drake, I'm seeing all the signs from eight years ago. The stress, the long hours, the dark circles under her eyes. At least this time she has Finn and Jessica. They are the ones taking care of her. Making sure she eats. Making sure she gets home every night. But today she came into the office smelling so bad I had to spray her down with air freshener before a meeting. Her arms were trembling from exhaustion. I asked her what was the matter, but she said nothing. *Nothing*, Drake. You do know when a woman says nothing is the matter, it's the complete opposite, right?"

"Yes, I do know that. When I saw her last night I noticed the exhaustion. I fed her dinner and tucked her into bed. She was gone when I woke up. What's going on, Shirley?"

"Shouldn't you know? You're her boyfriend, aren't you?"

The question hit him hard. He was and he had no idea what had pushed her this far. The damn file on Chord had been sitting on his desk for a week, but he'd been so occupied with correcting the IP address program for the government that he hadn't even been paying attention to it or to what was going on with Elle. He just assumed after the press conference two weeks ago everything was fine. Sure she was working long hours, but so was he. If she needed help, surely she would have asked him . . . right?

Drake ran his hand over his face. "Something bad is going on and I've been so caught up in my work I haven't bothered to find out what it is."

"Don't feel bad, dear. Elle doesn't ask for help. She didn't ask for it eight years ago, and she's not going to ask for it now. I may be a tough old broad, but I'm not in my eighties anymore. I can't be there for her like I've done in the past. She needs you now. She needs your love and unwavering support to make sure she comes out of the trench she's put herself in."

"Tell me everything I need to know," Drake ordered, his face set in sheer determination.

Chapter Seventeen

D rake walked Shirley to the elevator an hour later. His mind was reeling with what had been going on for the past weeks. Why hadn't Elle told him about the identity theft? *Because relationships need work,* he thought. It's not enough to passively be there for her. They needed to talk—more than just a "how was your day?" before landing in bed together. Sure, sex was important, but he wasn't with her for that reason. He was with her because their hearts were connected. And when the woman he loved was in pain, he should have put in the effort to find out why.

No wonder she looked exhausted last night. She was fighting for her company and now someone was out for her identity. Drake motioned Phillip into the office as he passed by his desk. Drake would watch the situation to see if he needed to buy up some shares of Titan Industries. The sooner Elle put this to rest, the better. He wouldn't tell her what he was doing. In fact, he hoped she'd never learn of it and that he'd never need to buy the stock to help her. It was just a contingency in case it looked like they would pursue diluting the stock.

"Phillip, after you have that stock ordered, clear my schedule for the rest of the afternoon."

Drake grabbed his coat and headed for the elevator.

Shirley was right; he should have known something was going on. He had Phillip's report on Chord and Titan Industries sitting on his desk, but he'd been so caught up in work that he hadn't followed through on his vow to help take them down. He made a mental note to send his investigator to the bank as well. He just hoped Mallory played nice. But if it was to help Elle, he was sure she would.

Damn it! When he noticed how tired she was, he should have found out why. It was one thing to be excited about his project, but quite another to ignore what was going on in her life. It wasn't just him anymore. He was part of an *us* now and he intended to never forget that again.

Elle's eyes burned as she tried to read the report in front of her. The meeting with Bellerose was tonight and she needed to read all the financials on the company beforehand. Allegra had been right: it was a good company to invest in. The trouble was she was using a lot of their capital to beat Titan Industries at their own game.

She pulled up Simpson Steel's records and ran her irritated eyes over the numbers. If they could collect the second payment on the new project Bree was working on, then they could afford a good-sized deposit on Bellerose. She'd already talked to Mr. Burger who had been more than happy to set up a business loan for the rest.

Rubbing her eyes, she looked back at the numbers and waited for them to come into focus. After Monday, this thing with Chord would be over and she could work at paying them off with capital from Titan. Mallory purchased her shares a couple days ago and Finn, yesterday. Jessica was meeting with a broker at that moment and purchasing hers.

During her research she found out both Simpson Global and Titan Industries shared a number of shareholders who were more than happy to tell Elle they disapproved of Titan hiring Chord McAlister and would eagerly vote in favor of the takeover. After all, Elle had proven to them over the years she could make them money, and lots of it. That was how she found out Chord was presenting his final plan of attack for Simpson Global on Monday at eight in the morning. She had set up a vote of Simpson Global shareholders that afternoon. He thought he had the Simpson shareholders in his pocket and was ready to call a vote.

"Elle."

Her head shot up and she realized she'd dozed off. She didn't know for how long, but, since she was still holding the financial reports in her hand, it couldn't have been too long.

"Drake," she said as she smiled. Elle wanted nothing more than to crawl into his arms at that moment. He had a way of making her forget everything else that was going on and leave her feeling loved and safe.

"You should have told me about Titan trying to force the buyout and about the identify theft. I called Mallory and our investigators are working with the bank. But more than that, I'm sorry. I'm so sorry, Elle."

"Sorry about what?" Elle's mind was still foggy. Investigators? Titan?

"I'm sorry I haven't been here for you. I thought you were just working hard. But then I find out you're in the middle of a hostile takeover while someone is out there pretending to be you. I should have been by your side."

Elle shook her head trying to clear the cobwebs. "It's okay. It's just business."

"You're my business, Elle. You come first. Please, tell me what I can do."

"Nothing. That's the thing. There's nothing you can do. I have to take him down. I have to deal with all this."

"Not alone you don't. You're exhausted. Let me take you home and put you to bed. We'll tackle this in the morning, together. Always together from now on."

Elle sighed. It sounded lovely. It just wasn't possible. "It's okay. You have your own company with your own problems."

"And successes. We just completed a program that will change the landscape of criminal investigations. We're a couple, we need to start sharing our ups *and* our downs. Come on, let me take you home and you can tell me everything that is going on."

"I can't. I'm sorry. I have all these things to get done today." Elle gestured to the folders and pink memo slips that covered her desk. "And I have a meeting tonight. Allegra has a major deal that will really bring Simpson Fashions into a whole new sphere. Besides getting all this done, I have to read this report and develop a plan of action for the purchase of it."

"Who is she looking at buying? Shouldn't she be handling it?"

"Bellerose. Owned by David Bell and Josh Rose. And no, I handle all negotiations. She's brought it this far and now I'll take it from here. Then she picks it back up once everything is signed on the dotted line. I've found it keeps relationships between them and their subsidiaries cleaner. When the VPs start working with the previous owners, there is no tension. They negotiated with me, not Bree or Allegra, and won't hold them responsible for any tense negotiating."

"How long until the meeting?"

"Five hours, why?"

"Elle, do you trust me?"

"Of course I do."

"Then find an empty office and study the report. Take your notes, write down the strengths and weaknesses, and do whatever it is that you need to focus on. Let me take care of everything that comes up for the next four hours and help you with what I can to clear your desk. I wrapped up my government contract and the team is working on smaller projects. I'm not needed this afternoon. Let me help you. If it can wait, it'll be sitting on the desk waiting for you. If it's time-sensitive, I'll handle it." Elle started to protest but Drake held up his hand. "If I need you, I'll come get you. I promise. But you need to ace this meeting tonight."

Elle sat still staring at Drake. She didn't really know what to say. Part of her mind tugged her toward the couch in the empty office next door. She could sit down and really study Bellerose without any interruptions. Let him help you, her mind whispered. But she'd never left anyone else in charge of Simpson Global before, even for just a couple hours. *Do you trust me?* Drake had asked. She didn't need to think about it any more. She had her answer.

"Okay." Elle felt secure in her decision. She was so tired and it would be a huge relief to spend whatever energy she had on her acquisition. She did trust him and he'd take care of her, her family, and her company as if they were his own.

Drake crossed the room and she looked up into his blue eyes and saw his love for her. "Come here, sweetheart," he whispered.

As Drake's arms came around her, a pleasured sigh escaped. He was so warm, so strong, so sure of himself. It gave her the confidence to let him help her while she focused on Bellerose.

Drake walked Elle down the hall as Jessica stood with wide eyes at the display of affection. He nudged the empty office door open with his foot and crossed to the leather couch. Elle was already half asleep, her face buried in his shoulder.

"Are you sure you can focus enough to work?"

"Yes. You just smell really good and are so warm," Elle sighed.

"Okay, I know exactly what you need. You've heard of carb loading, right? Well, we're going to caffeine load enough to get you through your meeting." Drake turned to Jessica standing in the doorway. "Think you can help with that, Jessica?"

"Sure do. We'll start slow, an espresso, and work our way up to a triple." Jessica shot them a grin and hurried off down the hall. Drake reached for Elle. His fingers traced the curve of her cheek as he pushed a loose piece of hair behind her ear.

"Anything particular you want me to start on?" Drake asked.

"So, you're my assistant for the day? You'll do whatever I tell you to?" Elle asked in a seductive voice.

"Anything and everything," Drake's low voice rumbled.

"Then fix my computer network," Elle purred before they both dissolved in laughter.

"Here you go! One espresso with a chocolate cupcake as a side," Jessica called out as she sailed into the room looking confused as Drake and Elle tried to stop laughing.

"Thank you." Elle said as she took some deep breaths and turned back to Drake. "I think I'm too exhausted to be funny, but thank you for helping me today. Jessica, take Drake to my office and let him handle all of the little things for a few hours."

"Handle?"

"That's right. Drake will be handling some of the business today while I work on the Bellerose deal. Your job is to keep me stocked with caffeine and help Drake as much as you can when I don't need you for this deal," Elle smiled. Her assistant was amazing at finding out interesting tidbits for her.

"You're a good friend, Jessica. Thank you for any help you can give me," Drake said sincerely. "But, now we have some work to do."

Jessica stared up at him as if he were from Mars, but then shook her head and got her game face on. "Let's do it."

Drake walked back into Elle's office and sat down behind her desk. "What can I do to help Elle?"

"Bree dropped this off for review," Jessica said as she placed a folder on the desk. "And these are all housekeeping issues that need to be handled."

Drake stared at the memo sheets as Jessica gave him a challenging look. "She does all this in a day?"

"Yes siree. And I have some things here to go over," Shirley said as she pushed her way into the office. "Good to see you came to your senses. Now, leave those reports here, Jess, and put all calls, emails, everything through. Mr. Charles is going to do some real work for once."

Drake felt a smile spread across his face as Shirley took a seat across the desk from him.

"Okay then. I have a stack of calls for you. I'll bring them in."

Shirley smiled at him and Drake felt like a hero. There was no greater feeling than helping the woman you love.

He ran his own company; how hard could it be to run Elle's for a couple hours?

Drake was on the verge of tears. He was man enough to admit that. He was going to cry. He ran his hand through his hair, making it stick up in all directions. It had only been three hours and he'd done more than he'd done at Drake Charles Enterprises for the last week. How did Elle do it? He was reading reports on steel production, shipping, building, and summarizing them for Elle to read later. He'd returned phone calls to every department under the sun within Simpson Global. He'd talked to accounting, legal, and human resources . . . at least he aced the call with the tech department.

Somehow Elle was able to handle rapid-fire questions from Bree, Allegra, and Jessica all while reading reports, talking with banks, and negotiating deals. Then came the report from Reid on the casinos in Europe and his plans for expansion. Who knew Reid had a brain? He was just like Phillip. So easy-going you'd forget they were some of the smartest people he knew. But one conclusion he came to easily was Elle really needed another vice president to handle all the financial institutions so she could focus on orchestrating each arm of Simpson Global.

"Elle, I was thinking about this morning . . . Whoa, you're not Elle." Drake hung up the phone with purchasing and looked up at Finn.

"No, I'm not. What about this morning?" Drake had never experienced jealousy before. It was a new feeling. He didn't particularly like it, but the thought of waking up alone this morning while Elle was with another man twisted something inside of him.

"Um, nothing to worry about. Where's Elle?" Finn asked.

"Working on the Bellerose deal. What were you doing this morning with Elle?" Finn didn't miss the hardness to his voice.

"After working out together this morning, I heard her talking on the phone in the car about something and had an idea I wanted to run by her," Finn told him vaguely.

"What do you mean, working out together?"

Finn suddenly narrowed his eyes. "Look, Mr. Charles, I don't know what you're doing here, but I think I'll talk to Elle. If she's not telling you things, then that's enough for me to know to keep my mouth shut."

Drake ran his hand through his hair again. One thing he'd learned from the past three hours is the employees of Simpson Global were fiercely loyal to the Simpson ladies. Drake let out a long breath.

"I'm sorry, Finn. I didn't mean to imply—well, I did, but I shouldn't have done it. Elle is preparing for that dinner tonight and doesn't want to be disturbed. I offered to cover her duties for a few hours."

"You, take over?" Finn tried not to laugh. "How's that going for you? Enjoying the fashion part?"

"Incredibly, especially the part where I got to look over the models' contracts. It included pictures." Drake grinned.

"Get out!" Finn stepped forward with a grin on his face and took the seat Shirley had vacated an hour ago.

"So, tell me about the working out and the problem."

Finn looked him over for a minute and finally gave a nod of his head. "I've been teaching her self-defense. She's going to bring Chord down very publicly and she wanted to feel confident that if he grabbed her again she could take care of herself."

Drake let out a long breath. "Good. Thank you, Finn. Now what's the problem?"

"One of the banks Simpson Global owns made a loan to P&P Agency. P&P can't pay it. They're going to go under by the end of this year."

"Really? How do you know that?"

"Kane Royale is a friend of mine."

"He's the wide receiver for the Atlanta Golden Eagles, right?" Drake asked about the state's most famous professional football player.

"Yes, but more interestingly, he's represented by P&P Agency. We work out at the same gym. Elle actually met him yesterday. Anyway, I had lunch with him today and he told me the agents are leaving in droves. He's going to be looking for a new agency by the end of the year, if not sooner."

"So . . ." Drake said slowly. He wasn't sure where Finn was going with this.

"So, I took the bar exam in December and I found out last week that I passed. That's why I was having lunch with Kane. To celebrate."

"You're a lawyer? Congratulations," Drake said in total surprise. He had no idea Finn had been in school.

"I sure am. I took night and online classes for the past four years. Elle encouraged me. Anyway, Kane said something that got my attention. He said, 'I wish you could be my agent.' He was joking, but it got me thinking. Why couldn't I be? I mean, I played professionally and I understand how professional sports work from a player's point of view. Plus I've seen what people have done that worked and what hasn't. I think I could be a good agent," Finn said passionately.

"Are you quitting?" Drake prayed he wasn't. He didn't know how he would break that to Elle.

"No. I would never leave Simpson Global. I want Elle to look into bringing P&P Agency under the Simpson Global brand name. I have all these plans running through my mind. I think we could make some big bucks off it."

Drake let out a relieved breath. "It's a promising idea. Especially if you branch out to entertainment as a whole." Finn's smile went from ear to ear. "However, for Elle to really look into it, she needs reports. Data, figures, assets, liabilities. Get it?"

Finn's smile faded.

"If you really want to take this seriously, then go talk to Kane and find out why he chose P&P. Research them and find out who else they represent. Then, see this?" Drake held up Allegra's initial report on Bellerose. "You need to do this."

Finn took it and started reading through it. The further he read, the more his brow furrowed. "This is a lot."

"Sure is. I would also recommend talking to some agents to get a feel for the business. It's pretty cutthroat from what I understand. Maybe Kane can get you an internship."

Finn nodded his head. "That's a great idea, Mr. Charles. I can intern at the same times I had previously taken my law classes. I'm sure Elle would agree."

"Well, I think it's a good idea. I'll go to bat for you, but I'm sure Elle will have some questions as well."

"Elle, are you . . . Whoops. Hi, Drake. Finn. What are you guys doing here?" Allegra asked as she stopped in the middle of the room, holding a garment bag and some sort of black case.

"Elle's preparing for the Bellerose meeting. I'm filling

in."

"You?"

"Yes. Excellent report on Bellerose, by the way. I'll go get Elle so you can help her get ready." Drake rose and headed out of the office, hearing Finn ask if Allegra would mind answering some questions on how to write those reports she gave to Elle. Good, he wasn't giving up. Finn had a good idea. Drake would be interested to see if he followed through on it.

Chapter Eighteen

Elle was wired. She had memorized the whole report and found out everything there was to know about Bellerose and its owners. She was prepared to casually slip the knowledge into their conversation and would be prepared to answer any questions as they came up. One of the arts to negotiating was to be so casual they didn't even know she was planting ideas and terms into the conversation.

"Is it time already?" Elle asked as she stretched.

"Yep. Allegra is in your office with . . . stuff for tonight. Looks very girly. How are you feeling?"

"Much better. Thank you for letting me prepare. Were there any crises?" Elle rubbed cramped neck and stood up.

"Let's see. First, I don't know how you do it. Twenty different things were going on all at the same time. I handled one of your tech issues. I returned most of your phone calls within the company and handled those with Shirley's help. I looked over the models' contracts for the fashion show Allegra is producing. I summarized Bree's report. And Finn passed the bar exam."

Elle jumped up and did a little happy dance while Drake stood up smiling at her obvious excitement. "I'm so happy for him. He's been working so hard on that."

"Well, he came armed with a suggestion. He had lunch

with Kane Royale. He's the . . ."

"Wide receiver for Atlanta," Elle finished. She'd met him the other morning at the gym. "What's the suggestion?"

"Kane informed him that P&P could go under by the end of the year. Agents are leaving in droves and Kane is looking for someplace new after the season is over."

Elle nibbled on her lip as she thought it through. "We have a loan out to them for a pretty big chunk. I wonder if I forgave the loan in trade for controlling interest of the company . . . Kane's contract has to be worth enough to make me think about it. Only what would I do with a sports agency?"

"Finn has some ideas. So do I for that matter. He wants to become an agent and is going to look for an internship and talk to some of his buddies. If the numbers allow, then I'd take it and expand it to an entertainment agency. There's lots of music, television, film, models . . . all here in Atlanta. Finn's going to put together a proposal for you."

Elle was impressed. She knew Finn had potential for so much more. She was so glad he finally found something to bite into. "I'll look into it. You did really well."

She linked her arm with Drake and leaned into him as they turned into the hallway. It lifted her heart to know she was with someone she could trust.

"We have a problem," Jessica shouted as she hurried down the hall.

"Shouldn't you be home?"

Jessica waived the question off. "I called to confirm dinner with Bellerose earlier today and had to leave a message. Remember how you said you wanted a casual dinner first to break the ice with them? Well, David Bell just called to say how excited he and Josh were for a date night and how they appreciated a chance to get to know you better before talking numbers."

"Isn't that a good thing?" Elle asked, slightly confused about the panicking.

"He also said how excited Josh was to meet Drake. Apparently Josh has a bit of a tech side and totally geeked out assuming Drake was going to be there since I told them it was a casual dinner."

Jessica didn't need to say anything more. Elle cringed and looked up at a very amused Drake. "I don't suppose you'd do me one more *teensy-weensy* favor, would you?"

"Let me guess. Romantic dinner with you and the men of Bellerose? At least I'll get to let my inner nerd out. Sounds like fun, but I'm a little underdressed." Drake looked down at his jeans and black sweater and shrugged.

"I can fix that," Allegra called from down the hall. "But you better move it. I've sent Finn to get some clothes from my office. With a little styling, I can make you the belle of the ball. Now hurry up, you two, this fairy godsister doesn't have a magic wand."

Drake chuckled and Elle gently pressed her hand to his arm. "Would you really do this for me? You've done too much for me already today and if it makes you uncomfortable to be a . . . well, a . . ."

"Worshiped tech nerd," Drake said dryly.

"I'm so sorry, but yes," Elle giggled. "I would totally understand if you want to skip it. I could make up an excuse for you, no problem."

"Sweetheart, I'm secure enough with myself to stand the thought of you using me as your personal nerd." Drake lowered his head and she felt his lips next to her ear. "Just as long as you promise to use me when we get home tonight."

Elle flushed as he whispered a few of the ways she could use him after dinner. She was just thankful Jessica rushed back to help Allegra and didn't see the way she suddenly forgot to breathe.

"Come on, you two," Allegra called as she grabbed a handful of items from Finn.

Drake pulled away and Elle forced herself to remember how to walk as she watched Drake saunter down the hall.

Elle slid her hand into Drake's as they drove through downtown Atlanta. The city seemed to twinkle with the glow of lights reflecting off the buildings' windows. Allegra had decked them both out in simple yet elegant attire for the night. The European cut of Drake's suit showed off his wide shoulders and narrow waist while the white dress shirt, left casually unbuttoned at the neck, showed his laid-back side.

As she snuggled against his chest and listened to his heartbeat, she realized she'd been so distracted with Chord that she'd missed the time to just be together with Drake. And she felt silly for feeling as if she couldn't talk to Drake about what was going on. She had just felt it was her problem and she had needed to deal with it. When they were together, she didn't want to focus on the bad, only the good. What a mistake that had been. She'd learned her lesson and would share everything with Drake from now on. He showed he'd help her, support her, or just hold her like he was now.

"I'm sorry I've been so preoccupied," she murmured as she nuzzled against him.

"I've been the same way. I was taking advantage of the fact you'd be around and didn't think how much time we were really together. And it's going to happen. We're both incredibly busy, but I realized it's not the amount of time we spend together, but the quality of it. I want to make you a promise. No matter what I'm doing, I will always step away to answer your call. Even if it's to tell me Shirley is eavesdropping again." Drake grinned down at her. "I'm always going to be there for you. And I always want to know what's going on with you. I love you, Elle."

"I love you, too." She wrapped her arm around his waist and gave him a hug. "I guess I'm just getting used to being a couple. I've been responsible for everything for so long, I'm used to depending only on myself. But today you showed me what being a couple is about. Thank you for looking out for me and for my company. You didn't have to do that."

"It's what I wanted to do. You're my everything. And after today I'm even more in awe of you. How you manage all the branches of the company and control the financials is beyond me."

Elle smiled against Drake's shirt. She was proud of herself and proud of her company. Hearing Drake's praises made her feel so good about all her hard work. Chord or this woman trying to steal her identity would never change that. "I've found myself thinking about the future lately. Usually when I'm on some conference call and everyone is arguing. I think about handing off more of the financial side. I've even considered bringing Jessica into the financial side so I can have a chance to experience life a little more. I get this vision of us together. I know men don't like to talk about the future, but it brings me sanity when things go crazy."

"I admit I used to be like that. If a woman mentioned the future, I would run and hide. Of course, it's all my mother can talk about. But this is different. You're different.

161

I think about those things as well. How it would be to come home to you every night. Think about finding a house that's just ours. Think about having you by my side for the rest of my life. Having children, fighting, loving, growing. I think about it all, Elle, with you and only you."

His images of their life became hers as Elle looked into Drake's eyes. He leaned down and caressed her lips with his. The tenderness of the kiss made Elle sigh as Drake tucked her head under his chin and gathered her in his arms to hold her.

All too soon the limo came to a stop in front of the restaurant. As the door opened, they both reluctantly pulled apart. For just a while it had been as if they were the only two people in the world. Drake eased out of the door and turned, offering Elle his hand. She placed her hand into his and decided to do exactly what David and Josh were doing—make this a date night.

Drake didn't let go of Elle's hand as they made their way to the table in the back of Atlanta's hottest new restaurant. David and Josh were already seated, sipping wine and laughing at something. This should be interesting. He felt as if he received a crash course on fashion and more specifically, Bellerose, today. He hoped he didn't make any faux pas.

"Oh. My. Gosh. As I live and breathe, it's Drake Charles," the young man, dressed in a hip navy blue suit and a lilac tie, cried.

Drake reached over the table and shook his hand. "You must be Josh. It's nice to meet you. This is my girlfriend, Elle Simpson." Drake placed his hand on Elle's back while she shook his hand.

Elle smiled at the blue-eyed man with floppy blond hair

who couldn't be more than twenty-five. While David Bell appeared to be the same age as Josh, he was more muscled with dark brown hair and brown eyes. He also wasn't practically crawling over the table to get to Drake.

"Hi, David. It's nice of you to have dinner with us tonight."

"It's our pleasure," David said quietly, but with a sincere smile on his face as he shook her hand and then Drake's.

Elle took her seat between David and Drake, but was quickly shut out of Drake's discussion as Josh started in on binary coding and a bunch of other words that were foreign to her.

"I tried to warn that nice secretary of yours, but Josh was a software engineer before we made it as designers. He still likes to mess around with it. In fact, he wants to build an app that lets people upload their picture to show how our clothes will look on them. He somehow wants to make it so the clothes fit the person's body shape. It's above me. I was a business major with a fashion minor. What about you?"

"Business and economics all the way. I knew from the moment I walked into my dad's little hole-in-the-wall office that I wanted nothing more than to run his company someday. We're family and there's nothing better than working with your family everyday." Elle smiled and thanked the waiter who poured her a glass of wine. Drake and Josh had pulled out their cell phones and were doing who knows what.

"That's nice. It's how we run Bellerose. Of course, with family there are always fights, too. They're not afraid to tell you when they think you're messing up." David's eyes crinkled as he smiled.

"My sisters love it when I mess up. They tease me relentlessly. But, they always have my back too."

"It's actually one of the reasons I agreed to meet. I met Allegra last year at a runway show. She was so carefree and full of life I immediately wanted to get to know her, because sometimes it's that easy to know someone is a good person. And she is. We've become acquaintances over the year. When I ran into her the other week and asked about you and Drake, she defended you before I'd even finished my question. It's obvious you're well-loved and respected by your family."

Elle held up her wine glass. "To families."

Drake and Josh looked up from their cell phones as if they were caught by the teacher for not paying attention in class. They raised their glasses and the whole table toasted.

Elle skipped into her apartment with her heels dangling from her fingers. Drake laughed as she twirled around. She had kept her cool all through dinner. She hadn't even overreacted as David and Josh looked at each other, and with a nod, asked if Elle had the paperwork to officially become part of Simpson Global.

But as soon as Finn safely tucked away the signed contracts and closed the door to the limo, Elle had lost it. She'd squealed, stomped her feet, and did a little dance in her seat. David and Josh enjoyed dinner so much with no pressure that they said they knew it was the perfect place for Bellerose.

"Thank you so much for being my tech nerd tonight." Elle threw herself into his arms and squeezed.

"It was no problem. Josh and I had a good time geeking

out, as you call it. Plus I remembered what was waiting for me when we got back home."

"Well, you do deserve a reward for helping land this contract." Elle stepped away and headed for the bedroom as she dropped her shoes and slid the zipper down the side of her dress.

Drake's mouth went dry as her dress slipped from her shoulders. She stopped at the door and with the sexiest little butt wiggle slid the dress off. God, he loved this woman. A woman who could close a multimillion-dollar deal and an hour later have him harder than steel with one little wiggle.

Elle ran her hand over Drake's chest. She played with the light sprinkling of hair before trailing her fingers along the smooth ridges of his abdomen. It was late, but after drinking all that caffeine and the high from dinner, she wasn't ready to go to sleep. As she felt the warmth of his muscles, she was actually thinking of a repeat performance.

"Hmm. That feels good," Drake sighed as her fingers dipped under the sheet.

"It's fun to explore you in the dark." Elle wisped her fingers along his upper thigh, teasing him.

"You know what happens to naughty girls, don't you?" Drake's hand ran down her spine softly and he gave her a light smack on her bottom.

Elle leaned back into his touch but instead of a moan, a scream escaped from her throat as the world came shattering down around her.

The door to her bedroom crashed open. Pieces of splintered wood flew through the air as men with guns stormed in. Drake flung himself on top of her pushing the breath from her lungs as Elle was pressed into the mattress.

"Secret Service! Hands up. Get your fucking hands up!"

Elle stopped screaming when she heard them identify themselves as Secret Service. She tried to put her hands up, but Drake refused to budge from where he pressed her nude body into the mattress. Out of the corner of her eye she saw four men encircle the room with guns pointed.

"Hands up! We will shoot you if you don't get your hands up and get out of bed slowly," one of the agents yelled.

"I will gladly get up, but I will not move until you pass my girlfriend some clothes," Drake responded tightly.

Elle tried to push him off her. When government agents were pointing guns at you, you should probably do as they say. However, Drake refused. He kept her covered. In fact, she was so covered she was finding it hard to breathe. From her position under Drake, Elle held out her hands as best she could and after some murmuring felt a lump of silk land on her hand.

"Thank you," she tried to call out from her mouth's place against Drake's bare chest.

She pulled the navy robe over her breasts and only then did Drake raise his hands and step naked from bed. Elle scrambled to cover herself with the robe as Drake straightened up and faced the agent at the door.

"Elle Simpson, you're wanted by the Secret Service. Put on the robe, we're taking you in for questioning. And here's our search warrant for your house and your office," the agent by the door told her as he held up the warrant. With a nod of his head, the other agents started to tear apart her room. It was then she saw more agents in her living room taking her computer and opening drawers.

"What's going on?" Drake asked. "What is she being taken in for?"

"And you are?" the lead agent demanded rather than asked.

"Drake Charles, Elle's boyfriend."

The agent's lips thinned. "Put some clothes on—after you've been searched by Agent Rodrick. We have some questions for you, too."

The agent who threw Elle the robe was patting down Drake's suit and tossed him the pants and dress shirt.

"I'm sorry," Elle said as nicely as possible as she clung to her robe and slipped on her bunny slippers lying next to the bed. "But I don't understand. Why am I being questioned?"

"We'll talk at the office. Let's go."

Elle's heart beat hard against her chest. She had thought getting a speeding ticket was bad. That was nothing compared to the fear she was feeling now. The two agents at the door refused to lower their weapons and, as Elle stared at them open-mouthed, she realized they also weren't going to turn around. Elle turned her back as she slipped the robe on. As soon as she tied the belt, Agent Rodrick had her hands behind her back. Cold steel clasped tight against her wrists as the cuffs locked in place.

Chapter Nineteen

Elle paced the interview room in her robe and bunny slippers. A two-way mirror covered one of the light green walls enclosing the windowless room. A rectangular table with four chairs sat in the middle of the room. She'd been thrown in the small room as her request for an attorney fell on deaf ears. The agents kept insisting they were operating under protection of an executive order.

She'd been separated from Drake the second she tied her robe. Drake's threats to the Secret Service still rang in her ears from when they marched Elle from the condo and into the unmarked car.

Elle stopped her pacing when the door opened as the lead agent and Agent Rodrick entered. Agent Rodrick looked to be in his thirties with his rec-league athletic appearance. On the other hand, the lead agent looked to be in his late forties and still in good enough shape to throw a guy through a window. The only hints at his age were the small lines around his eyes and some stray gray hairs along his temples.

"Miss Simpson, I'm Agent Murphy. This is Agent Rodrick. And you're in serious trouble. Sit down and tell me everything right now and maybe you'll be able to walk out of jail before you're a senior citizen."

Elle sat, more like fell, into the chair. "What on earth do

you think I did?"

A piece of paper was shoved in front of her. "I know exactly what you did. You threatened to kill the President of the United States during her visit next week." Agent Murphy slid two pictures in front of her before she had a chance to read the piece of paper. "With this gun you bought last week."

Elle tried to stop the shaking in her hands, but couldn't, so she didn't even try to pick up the pictures. One was a picture of some kind of rifle. The second was a picture of her at a gun shop purchasing a rifle.

Drake pounded his hand against the table but got no reaction. No matter how loud he screamed or what he said, the agent wouldn't listen to him. He'd tried to reach Elle when they dragged her handcuffed from the condo, but he'd been slammed against the wall by two agents. Since then they hadn't seemed to care what he said.

"I'm telling you, Elle would never make threats against the President. She has no reason to do that."

"And I'm telling you, Mr. Charles, we have ironclad evidence. Emails, gun registration, and surveillance from the gun store. Your girlfriend is going away for a very long time. Now, the question is: will you be joining her?"

"Joining her?" Drake's head snapped back. Wait, was he being interviewed or interrogated? They'd asked him all about his business and all about his relationship with Elle. Did they really think he and Elle were in this farce together?

"That's right. Maybe you helped her. She's your girlfriend and you love her. You'd do anything for her, maybe even kill for her."

"Look, Agent . . ."

"Wallace."

"Look, Agent Wallace, Elle wouldn't do that. She's not that type of person. Neither of us has any reason to kill the President. While we're political in the sense that we vote, we're nowhere near the extremist type. Neither of us has even used our money to get any particular person elected. Furthermore, she's never mentioned anything against President Nelson. In fact, we both voted for her. Why would she want to kill her?"

"Her email suggested it was due to the stricter transparency in banking regulations. What do you know about that?"

"Quite a bit actually. Elle met with the old bank trustees a month ago or so. They were upset because *she* was putting more regulations on reporting from her banks than the government required." Drake stood back up and started pacing. He headed over to the two-way mirror and looked at his reflection. "Check it out. Her secretary will have records of it. The motive is bullshit because it's fake. She didn't do this."

He saw Agent Wallace rise behind him and pick up the file he was carrying. "I'll do just that. She's in an interview room down the hall. Along with Elle's family, friends, driver, and office manager. This is your last chance, Mr. Charles. Tell me what I want to know or when they tell me, and they will tell me, I'll hold you as an accomplice."

Drake turned around and looked Wallace in the eyes. "Go ahead. There's nothing to find. And watch out for Shirley; you're just her type."

Jessica couldn't feel her face. The blood had been drained for so long she was sure she'd never be able to smile again. Men in black jackets, black SUVs, and guns had shown up at her house to escort her to the downtown office of the

Secret Service in the middle of her night. Her husband had protested, her children had screamed, and Jessica hadn't been able to put together a coherent thought since.

"I'm sorry," she said flustered at the agent sitting across from her. He looked to be in his mid-thirties, but that was all she could tell as she stared down at her hands in her lap.

"It's okay. Take your time. It must be quite a shock to discover your boss was planning to kill President Nelson."

Jessica looked up from her entwined fingers and felt her heart start to beat again. "No, Agent Wallace. It's not that. I'm sorry that I can't believe such an asinine assertion. She wanted even stricter transparency in reporting. I have her notes from the meeting at the office. Elle Simpson is the best woman I know, and she'd never kill a person in cold blood. And I'm sorry," Jessica stood quickly, so quickly in fact she swayed a bit, "but I will not tolerate you saying this about her. I refuse to believe it, and I refuse to be part of this corruption."

Agent Wallace looked up at her and slowly slid a photo across the table. Jessica looked down at it and felt her stomach drop. It was Elle purchasing a rifle.

"Oh, fiddlesticks."

"Exactly. Would you care to amend your statement about Miss Simpson?"

"So, you've never been close with your cousin?" Mary heard the question and didn't quite know how to answer.

"I don't know. Yes. No. Kinda," she stammered. Mary had also been escorted from her mother's house to the Secret Service Office in the middle of the night. For the last ten minutes, the obscenely cute Agent Wallace had been asking her all sorts of questions about the family.

"Kind of? Because it sounds to me as if your cousin

hired you out of pity and only keeps you around as some sort of lackey. You just told me every time you try to talk to her, she's with her sisters or Miss Westin. So, how well do you really know your cousin?"

"I'm not a lackey," Mary said softly, but with steel to her voice. "I do more than Elle even knows about. She may not appreciate me, but I'm far smarter and more resilient than she gives me credit for being."

"I'm telling you, I don't care for one minute what that picture is. That is not my daughter," Margaret Simpson declared.

Agent Wallace sat back in his chair and Margaret stared him down. "And how do you know this is not your daughter?"

"I'm her mother, aren't I? I gave birth to her. I raised her and that is not my daughter. It's not one specific thing. I can just tell it's not her. A mother knows."

"And you think that will hold up in court and save her from a life in prison?"

"If there's one mother on the jury, then yes."

"How do you explain this email then?"

Margaret picked up a copy of an email and read it. Sure it said it came from Elle, but it wasn't her words. "I may just be an old woman, Agent Wallace, but even I know there are ways to hack email accounts. My daughter is a stickler for grammar and business terms. This threat is too fluffy and too dumb-sounding to be from her."

"Too dumb-sounding?"

"That's right."

"No evidence. Nothing to help with proving your daughter's innocence except you know that's not her in the picture because you're her mother. And she didn't write this letter because if she had, it would have been better written?" Agent Wallace asked with disbelief.

"That's right. And I have a trunkful of her writing at my house. I'm sure you're already looking through it, but you'll see. These aren't her words and that's not her. Meanwhile you're so focused on her, you're not looking for the person setting my daughter up. Did it ever occur to you that she is being framed? There's already been a PR attack against Elle and Simpson Global. Is it really that much of a stretch to think someone would do this to ruin my daughter and her company?"

Finn's hands curled into tight fists under the table. Agent Wallace was trying to be his friend and all he wanted to do was to slam his fist into the agent's face. Not that he wasn't being nice to Finn and simply doing his job. The agent wasn't doing anything illegal from what Finn could tell. But he still wanted to slam his fist into Agent Wallace for the things he was saying about Elle.

"She did it. She's going away for a long time. What I need to know is if she was planning it alone? Tell me about Drake Charles. When did they start seeing each other?"

"They met at Christmas. He's a good guy. He takes care of her. Something she's needed for a long time," Finn said as calmly as he could.

"You care about her?"

"Of course I do."

"Do you love her?"

"I do. I imagine I love her as much as one can love his sister. She encouraged me through school. She never thought of me as a has-been ballplayer. No, she saw me for me and supported my hopes and dreams. There is no way a woman like that would kill someone over politics. You're looking at the wrong person, Agent."

"Then how do you explain this?"

Finn picked up the picture and looked at it closely. Something about it nagged him, but he couldn't put his finger on it. "I don't care what this looks like. Elle wouldn't kill the President. But I do think you should talk to Hailey Duveaux. She was fired a couple months ago and is believed to have sent out a fake press release about Elle."

"Why was she fired?" Agent Wallace asked as he wrote something down on a pad of paper.

"Sleeping with clients. Elle found it degrading and completely unethical. She was fired instantly and has been bad-mouthing Elle ever since."

"Anyone else have a grudge against Miss Simpson?"

"Plenty. She's a force in changing the landscape of business. She wasn't raised with a silver spoon in her mouth, Agent Wallace. She worked for everything she has and she's done it at the side of her employees, not on their backs. And we love her for it. But others do not. She cares more about her employees' happiness and doing things right than anyone I know. How many employers provide daycare on-site so the employees can have lunch with their kids? So mothers can feed their babies throughout the day? How many employers reward their employees based on their merits and hard work, and not who they kiss up to? The harder you work, the better job you do, the bigger your bonus."

"She sounds like the perfect boss. Then who doesn't like her?"

"To get all the perks, you have to follow the rules. Anyone who violates our contract, like Hailey did, is immediately fired. Not many people have been, but the ones who cross the line are let go without severance. Then there's her competition. The old men out there don't appreciate a young lady coming in and doing their job better. Their best employees leave for Simpson Global once there's an opening and never look back. Then you have people like Chord McAlister who tried to take over her company only to be pummeled, figuratively, by Elle for daring to try it."

"Do you think President Nelson got in her way? If she pummeled this Chord guy, what's stopping her from doing it to the President?"

"I said, figuratively. Elle ruined his career and took over the company that had tried to oust her. She didn't beat him up. In fact, he's the one that grabbed her hard enough to leave bruises the other week. No, if President Nelson crossed Elle, she wouldn't be dead. She'd be packing up her belongings and moving out of the White House, alive."

Bree sat at the table with her legs and arms crossed. She dangled her heel off her toe as she listened to Agent Wallace accuse Elle of threatening to kill President Nelson. It didn't make sense. Elle would never do something like that. She believed in using her words, not weapons. Agent Wallace seemed to blow off her statement that Elle wanted more transparency and more record keeping when it came to banking than the bill President Nelson had recently signed. No matter what she said, Agent Wallace was twisting it against her sister.

He threatened her and accused her of being an accomplice. But after the letters she got in the mail, his threats didn't cause her to blink an eye. So, she sat calmly and listen to him accuse her sister, Drake, and herself of this ridiculous set-up.

Then when she tried to help by offering another

suspect, he'd acted as if she hasn't said a word. He'd completely ignored her suggestion to look into Hailey and now her patience was at an end as she tried to tell him about the bank fraud.

"I'm telling you, a woman who looked just like Elle tried to clean out two million dollars the other week. Just call First Peachtree and talk to the officer there."

"Or maybe it was just your sister getting her cash ready to take out the President. Your sister did this. We have more evidence than we need to put her away and all you can say is that you know she didn't do it?"

"That's right. Oh, and you can kiss my ass." Bree shot Agent Wallace a cold grin as he simply stood up and walked out the door shaking his head.

Mallory smiled sweetly at the agent as he took a seat across from her at the table. Out of habit, she ran her finger over her great-grandmother's pearls and waited to destroy the son of a bitch who dared hold her best friend for a crime she didn't commit. But through her years in security, she found the best way to learn things from men was to act like a simpering mess. She didn't understand it, but it worked. It also scared the dickens out of them when she turned serious.

"Miss Westin, you're Miss Simpson's best friend and head of security," Agent Wallace started again. He'd been talking for thirty minutes, laying out different allegations. "How did you not see this coming or did you help her purchase this weapon?"

Mallory looked at Agent Wallace and smiled again. She even threw in a bat of her eyelashes. "First off, Agent Wallace," Mallory's soft Southern voice floated melodically through the air, "Elle would never shoot the President.

Secondly, if I were helping her, I wouldn't have her buying a twenty-two rifle. For crying out loud, that's such a weak gun you'd be better off using a paintball gun."

"So you know your guns?"

"You do know I run a security firm, right? I would hope the Secret Service would be able to figure that out." Mallory batted her lashes again and smiled.

"We just figured you 'ran' a company your daddy bought you like so many other bored socialites."

Mallory tossed her head back and laughed. "Oh, Agent Wallace. I'm so disappointed in you. Your research on me is just as shoddy as on the picture. A picture that looks surprisingly familiar to video captured by First Peachtree of a woman claiming to be Elle trying to steal millions of dollars."

"Or of Elle setting up her escape cash for after she shot the President."

"Elle has bank accounts all over the world. She has way more than two million dollars at hand. If she really wanted to escape, she could pull together a lot more money than that. Now, let me tell you what's going on."

"You think you know?"

"I think I have a better grasp on it than you."

"Do tell."

"Someone is out to destroy Elle and Simpson Global. What better way than the press release, the attempted theft, and when none of that worked, having the Secret Service arrest her. Funny. Normally the Secret Service doesn't allow pictures to be taken at the time of arrest."

"What are you talking about?"

"As you know, my daddy, the senator, knows a picture can take you down. So what better way than to have the Secret Service arrest your competition? All you need is the picture. It doesn't even matter if you're innocent. The damage is already done. A friend at the six o'clock morning news just sent this to me. They're running it in a segment set to start in five minutes."

Mallory slid her phone across the table to show Agent Wallace his picture and other agents escorting Elle from her building in the middle of the night. Gone was the southern belle, gone was the ditzy socialite, and in its place was a tight and strong voice with a demeanor to match. "You might want to have them pull that, since it's identifying agents and all."

Agent Wallace leapt from the table and hurried from the room.

Shirley's head nodded and her chin fell to her chest. She'd been sitting too long and decided to just rest her eyes. Images of hunky half-dressed Secret Service agents filled her mind. They were ripping off their shirts as they danced around her. One reached out and caressed her arm. She may be old, but there was still fire in the furnace. Oh yeah, he could touch her all he wanted!

The agent shimmied and then reached out and placed his fingers to her neck. "Oh, thank God. She's alive."

That wasn't a sexy thing to say. Shirley tried to rewind the dream and have him touch her someplace else when she was shaken awake. Her eyes popped open and one of the agents from her dream appeared before her.

"Damn," Shirley sighed.

"Sorry, what was that, ma'am?"

"I said, 'Damn.' I was hoping you'd be naked." The agent's face went blank and he stood staring at her for a moment. "Well, are you going to start talking or should I get back to dreaming about you naked and dancing for me?"

The agent straightened up. "Excuse me for a second," he mumbled before heading back out the door.

"Hmph. Woke me up for nothing," Shirley complained to herself.

A minute later, the door opened again and the agent walked purposefully in the room and took a seat across from her at the table.

"So, sonny, have you decided if you're talking or dancing yet?" Shirley asked him as she looked him over. He'd do. Not as handsome as her late husband, God rest his soul. But that didn't mean she wouldn't enjoy seeing him rip his shirt off and shake his gun about. It'd been a real long time since she'd seen one of those, well, except on the internet.

"Talking. We're talking. I'm Agent Wallace. I just have a couple quick questions. What would Elle do if someone made her mad?"

"Mad? How so? I mean she deals with pig-headed old coots every day. They make her mad, but she usually just keeps her head down and does her job better than them and shoves it politely down their country club throats. Now, if she really gets mad, she turns into her mother."

"I don't know what that means. But I have met her mother."

"Then you know. She gets that look and tightens her lips a little and then proceeds to lecture them like they are dumber than dirt."

"Ah, got it." Wallace laughed as she saw the blush stain his cheeks. "Has she ever been violent? I know she's taking self-defense lessons."

"Only because that shitbag, excuse my French, of an ex-boyfriend is back and the last time she saw him, he grabbed her. She didn't like feeling helpless. But, she doesn't own a gun and wouldn't even know how to shoot it if she had one in front of her. She's always used her words for her defense."

"I've heard about the bank and the theory that someone is impersonating her." He slid a picture across the table. "What do you think?"

Shirley looked at the picture. Something wasn't right. It looked like Elle, but it didn't at the same time. "I don't think that's her. I can't tell you why; it's just a feeling. But something's not right with it."

"Anyone new in her life or anything stand out to you from the past couple of months?"

"Well, she met Drake. She had to fire that hussy Hailey Duveaux for playing hide the salami with half of her clients. Besides that, it was nothing out of the ordinary until that press release came out. But my money is on Hailey. She was madder than a wet cat when she was fired."

"Thank you for your help. I'll be back in a while if I have any more questions."

"I have a question, Agent Wallace."

"Yes?"

"Are you married?" Shirley grinned to herself as the young agent shook his head and he hurried from the room. Poor boy, he'd be eaten alive by the women she grew up with.

Allegra Simpson sat quietly in the interview room. The blinds were open on the interior windows so she watched the agents as they worked at their desks. It wasn't like she could do anything else. It was almost seven in the morning and she had been sitting for hours waiting for Agent Wallace to get to her.

A nice agent who had brought her some coffee told her that Elle was under investigation for threatening to kill the President. It was stupidest thing she'd ever heard and was sure Elle would be waltzing out in no time. However, as she sat there for the past three hours, she hadn't seen Elle once and that worried her.

Finally a young man stopped outside the door and looked at a file. He looked up and out into the room. Allegra followed his gaze and saw Hailey strutting into the office in a skin-tight dress and five-inch heels. Hailey was flipping her hair and Allegra could see her fawning over the agents from across the room . . . and see them falling for it.

Allegra shot from her chair and ripped open the door. The agent reading the file nearly fell through the now-opened door, but caught himself before knocking her over.

"Where do you think you're going, Miss Simpson?"

"To have a word with the woman behind this."

The agent kept an impassive face but simply raised a brown brow out of amusement. "You think we're just going to let you see your sister?"

"Who said anything about my sister? No, I'm going to see that floozy over there making a puddle out of your agents. Real professional of them by the way."

"You think Miss Duveaux is behind this?"

"You bet I do. Look at them, pathetic. It's like the sight of breasts flips a switch in their heads and they revert to cavemen."

Men surrounded Hailey as she crossed her arms, pushing her breasts up for the agents' viewing pleasure.

"They're interviewing her."

Now it was Allegra's turn to raise an eyebrow in mock amusement. "Really? It takes four agents to interview her while I've been waiting three hours for one agent? That's it,

I'm calling my lawyer."

"Come in, have a seat first." Agent Wallace ushered her to a chair and sat down opposite her. "I promise you, they are interviewing her. They're allowing her to feel as if she's in control."

"Is that what you're doing? Trying to get me to feel a bond with you so I talk more openly?"

"Yes, but you're also the last person I have to interview and quite frankly, I have a feeling you aren't going to tell me anything I haven't already learned." Agent Wallace ran a hand over his face and sat back in his chair. "You're the fashion one, right?"

"Yes."

"And you know your sister would never do anything like this, right?"

"Right."

"Will it matter if I show you the picture of your sister buying the gun she threatened to shoot the President with?" Agent Wallace slid a picture across the table and Allegra looked down at it. She let out a long breath she didn't even realize she'd been holding.

"Scary to see this side of your sister, isn't it?"

"No, it's not that. This isn't my sister and I can prove it."

Agent Wallace sat up and placed his arms on the table. "How?"

"See these shoes? They're super cute, right?"

Agent Wallace looked at the picture. "They're black, pointy, and have a strappy thing around her ankle, so what?"

"They're this season's *it* shoe. They're over eight hundred bucks a pair. Why is this relevant? My sister wears heels but hates them with a passion. She calls them Satan's stilettos."

"I still don't get it."

"She kicks her shoes off every second she can. She would never, I mean, *never* own a pair of heels with straps around the ankles."

"Seriously? This is your proof?"

"Seriously. The ankle strap prevents her from kicking off the shoes. Check her closet, you won't find those shoes, and you won't find a single pair of heels with ankle straps."

Chapter Twenty

Agent Rodrick and Agent Murphy glared at Elle. They'd been firing off questions so fast that her head was spinning. She was beginning to get names, dates, and details confused. They'd been going so long that everything was becoming jumbled in her mind.

"You were mad at the regulations requiring transparency. You were mad that the President was going to cost you millions and you don't even remember what you were doing when this picture was taken?"

"Stop! Just stop," Elle cried. She tried to control her breathing as the agents looked on smugly. "I know what you're doing. You're trying to get me confused so I'll admit to this. Have you found Hailey Duveaux? I think she was the one who tried to ruin me in the press for firing her."

"Or maybe you're trying to destroy her for bad mouthing Simpson Global—just like you did to Chord McAlister."

The knock on the two-way mirror stopped Elle from having to respond, thank goodness. A headache of epic proportions was trying to crack her skull open, and the last thing she wanted to do was go into the humiliation of explaining about Chord yet again.

The agents stared her down for a minute and then she was finally left alone in the uncomfortable room. She crossed her arms on the table and placed her head on them. Elle had to be strong. She had to believe the truth would come out. If it was true that the Secret Service was talking to her family, friends, and co-workers, then they had to know by now that she wouldn't do this. What must everyone be saying? What was this doing to Simpson Global? Maybe it wasn't public knowledge yet. Maybe it would never be public and her company would be safe.

Elle tried to close her eyes and sleep while she waited, but adrenaline was still coursing through her body. Instead of sleeping, she kept her head on her arms and told herself over and over again that everything would be all right. For hours, she chanted her mantra over and over until the door finally opened.

Agent Murphy opened the door and stuck his head in. "Miss Simpson, come with me."

Elle rose and followed him out of the interview room and down the hall. She passed other interview rooms and wondered if Drake was in one of them. Before she made it to the office area, Agent Murphy opened another door and gestured for Elle to go in.

The room was a conference room, much like one at Simpson Global. There were five other agents, boards with papers posted on them, the table covered with her things, and a whole wall of dry erase board with her information and all her acquaintances on it. Arrows connected them along with references to pieces of evidence and photos that were attached by magnets.

"The Secret Service receives over nine thousand threats a year against the President, Miss Simpson. Some are easily filtered out. Others we have to investigate, especially when the President will soon be visiting."

"And you really think I would just send you a letter telling you when, where, and how I was going to kill her?" Elle said with disbelief.

"You wouldn't believe how stupid some people are. They call us and tell us all the details of their plans and why they're going to do it. Of course, there are also those who don't brag and we only find out because family turns them in. Then there are times they're overheard at a restaurant, or we hear from undercover agents or police. The point is, we have to figure out which of the nine thousand threats are actual threats that need to be stopped. This is Agent Wallace." Agent Murphy nodded to the young man who came to stand in front of Elle. "He's going to explain why your letter was deemed credible."

"Hi, Miss Simpson. If you don't mind, let me start at the beginning of our process so you can understand how we've arrived at our conclusion. First, this email was sent to the general White House contact email. A White House employee received it and sent it to us. An agent in D.C. ran a quick background on you and up popped the new gun permit application. Then they ran the IP address on the email and confirmed that it belonged to you. A full background was compiled and then sent to our local office here in Atlanta. We visited the gun shop and got surveillance of you buying the weapon. That was more than enough to bring you in."

"But I didn't do it. I didn't send that email," Elle practically shouted for the umpteenth time. She even threw in a frustrated foot stomp only to be embarrassed as her bunny ears swayed with anger. It was hard to be intimidating in bunny slippers.

"We believe you," Agent Murphy cut in. "But it took a while to look at all the evidence, compile the statements, and so on."

"Oh, thank goodness. So, have you found out who it is?" Elle was so relieved she felt as if she would collapse. Exhaustion hit her hard and fast as she watched the men look between them.

"We were hoping you could help us with that." Agent Wallace held out a chair and Elle took a seat.

"How? I told you everything I know."

"I need you to think about all the people you come into contact with. Is there anyone jealous of you on a personal or professional level?"

"Not that I know of. I mean, I'm sure some of the other competing businesses wouldn't cry if Simpson Global collapsed, specifically Titan Industries. But enough to do all this? They want to take my company over, not destroy it." As soon as she said Titan's name, an unknown agent started typing away on a laptop.

"What about your cousin?" Agent Wallace suggested.

"Mary? No. I mean, well, she's Mary. She's always been a bit of a whiner. And she sighs, a lot. And complains about, well, everything. But, she's family. She wouldn't do this. What would be the point?"

"She was pretty adamant that you underestimate her. Plus, she was very bitter that you don't include her in more business talks as you do with your sisters. I should also point out that from a distance, she looks a heck of a lot like you. Same size, body shape, hair color . . ."

Elle shook her head. "No way. Mary would never do that. Besides, she's not tech savvy enough to pull off a good fake I.D. and hack into my email to send these notes."

Agent Wallace nodded in agreement. "You're right, she's not. Let me ask you this. Is there anyone new in your life savvy enough with technology to pull this off? Someone she could be working with?"

"The only person I know besides my I.T. department smart enough to pull it off is Drake. Wait, you think she's working with Drake?"

"We do. Are you aware he just completed a project for the government that works to trace all IP addresses, even those being masked? And in addition to that work, he found a way to make any IP address impossible to trace? He says he closed the loop, but I'm sure he kept a back door open."

"I don't understand," Elle said slowly as her mind tried to process what Agent Wallace was telling her.

"Criminals use IP generators to hide the originating IP address—your digital identification so to say. Using an IP generator, I can sit here and use a stolen credit card, launder money, and send a threatening email to the President. When it's traced, it will appear to come from Belize or Somalia—get the picture?"

"And Drake found a way to get through the fake address and instead show that it's you here in Atlanta?" Elle asked.

"That's right. During the development of this software, he also figured out a way to be able to hide any IP address. So, it's not hard to believe he could have either hacked your computer when you were out of the office or simply found a better way to make us believe it was your IP address being used. Was he ever alone with your computer at the office?"

Elle thought back over the past couple of months. There had been numerous times she'd left him in the office with her things. Or when she brought home her laptop and then took a shower or went to work out. Still, it didn't feel right. "There were plenty of times, but it's too far-fetched. First, I trust him and even though Mary may get on my nerves, she's family and she wouldn't do this. I can't see them working together. And I don't understand for what purpose."

"You're in charge of a multibillion-dollar company and you wonder what the motive is for a cousin stuck in the shadows and dependent on you for a job? Mr. Charles could have easily exploited your cousin into helping him with the promise of letting her have a piece of the pie after he takes it over. How is it any different from what Chord McAlister did to you?"

Pain struck Elle's head and her stomach tightened as she pictured Drake using her in order to gain control of her company. Sure, she could imagine it. After all, Drake had sat behind her desk and run the company just a day ago. And Agent Wallace was right—she did push Cousin Mary off a lot.

The trouble was, no matter what story the Secret Service told her, no matter what kind of nightmare visions she was picturing, Elle's heart knew the truth. "No. Family is family and Mary wouldn't do it. It doesn't matter if she's bitter or if I didn't treat her as well as I should. She wouldn't do it. And Drake isn't anything like Chord. In my heart, I know it's the truth."

"Isn't that a bit naive of you? You're a smart woman. Use your head," Agent Murphy scolded.

"I know it's naive. I know what you must think of me, but I know it's not them. Have you looked into Hailey yet?"

Agent Wallace shook his head. "I wish it were otherwise, but we think it's them. We talked with Hailey and it's not her. She has an air-tight alibi for the time the gun was purchased."

"If her alibi is a man, she could have gotten him to lie

for her." No, it had to be Hailey. If it wasn't Hailey, then she would actually have to consider that it was someone close to her.

"Hailey has a new job at a high-class escort service. She was at a corporate function with the boss. His wife was out of town and she went as his *niece*. There's video surveillance and pictures in the society pages along with two hundred witnesses." Agent Wallace sat down next to her and took her hand in his. "You need to come to terms with the fact someone close to you is trying to destroy your career and is not above sending you to jail to do so."

"But . . . but, Mary surely has an alibi. It can't be her. I know it can't be."

"She doesn't. We checked your security logs at work and while it shows you were at the office, Mary was not. She doesn't scan back in until thirty minutes after the purchase of the gun. We've also worked this morning with Miss Westin and First Peachtree. Mary was similarly out of the office when this woman made an appearance at First Peachtree. You may not want to believe it, but it's worth us looking into further."

"She's family. I know that sounds strange since families have a long history of acting against each other, but not mine. You can look into her. But it's not her and it's not Drake. What's next? What do I need to do?"

"Your case is being changed from a threat against the President to a case of identity theft. Someone is out there trying to be you. I'd have Miss Westin put added security on you at all times. With your permission, we'd like access to every account you have. Here are our cards. We'll be in contact, but if you think of something, anything, you call us."

Elle took the cards and went to put it in her pocket only

to realize she was still in her robe. "Sure. I'll get you all the information on my accounts today."

Agent Murphy stood and looked down at her. "We'd also appreciate your complete confidentiality on this. I know your friends will want to know what happened, but you are not to mention the roles we think your cousin and boyfriend played. You may break up with him if you wish, or continue your relationship. Either way, be careful. Most identity thieves are someone close to you: boyfriends, roommates, co-workers, or neighbors. And Mr. Charles fits a couple of those categories."

"I may disagree with you, but I won't say anything."

Agent Wallace looked nervously at her and Elle wondered what more there could be. Whatever it was, she had a feeling it wasn't good.

"There's one more thing. Someone knew you were going to be arrested and snapped a picture of you coming out of the building this morning. It was about to run on one of the news stations. Luckily we got it pulled before it aired and told the news station that you were assisting us on an investigation. We've answered all inquiries and directed your secretary to do the same. So far there have only been a couple calls from the other stations that heard a rumor of your arrest. They seem to be leaving it alone after talking to us. We wanted to trace the photo, but it was a print copy dropped off at the station. We're trying to find out how it got there, but so far we haven't been able to get any leads."

Elle closed her eyes and felt like finding a hole to climb into. "They got exactly what they wanted then. With that picture—and it's out there now—I'll be ruined. Simpson Global will take a huge hit in the stock market and the deals we have lined up . . ."

"The Secret Service is standing by you, Miss Simpson.

That picture should never have been taken and we will make sure your name is cleared if it pops up anywhere else. If there's any trouble, call us and our office will take care of it. You're free to go. Agent Wallace can take you home, but I believe your family is still here and will probably want to do the honors."

Elle stood up slowly, keeping her hand clasped tight around the lapels of her robe. "Agent Wallace, do you think I'm in danger? I mean, this woman is trying to ruin me. Do you think she'll be upset when I walk out of here?"

Agent Wallace's eyes flashed as his face tightened just enough to give Elle the answer. She might have won the battle tonight, but the war being waged against her wasn't over.

Chapter Twenty-One

D rake stopped pacing the small lobby packed full of Elle's friends and family. Around nine that morning, they were all told they could leave. When he asked about Elle, he was told she was still talking to the agents. It seemed no one wanted to leave her, so they had all gathered in the small room and took turns pacing.

Mallory had told them about the photo delivered to the news studio. Jessica told them about Agent Wallace instructing her to tell any press that Elle was helping the Secret Service. Drake was relieved when he heard that news.

"That has to be good, right?" Margaret asked the room for the tenth time as they rehashed everything Agent Wallace said or asked.

"I just don't understand why he didn't tell me. I'm the head of public relations," Mary said with a sigh that sounded as if her cat had just been run over.

"Mary. You need to get a grip. This isn't about you. It's about Elle," Margaret snapped and Drake felt like clapping.

"It's always about Elle." Mary stomped her foot.

"Mary, I love you like a daughter. I've listened to every break-up, to every perceived slight made against you, to everything my kids are doing that you're not, and how unfair it all is. I've had enough. You are in charge of your life. If you don't like things the way they are, then change them. Take command of the PR department and then people won't bother Jessica with it. Take command of your life and men will stop walking all over you."

Margaret ignored the fish mouth Mary was making as she gasped for breath to reply.

"And you're right, today is about Elle. I daresay tomorrow will be as well. But when the time comes that you need us, we will be there for you. Why? Because we're family, even my stuck-up, snotty, whiny sister. And family sticks together."

"Well said, Mom."

Drake turned around and saw a very tired and pale Elle standing at the door. His heart sped up, and before he could stop himself he had her pressed against his chest.

"Um cmt brth . . ."

Drake looked around guiltily and released his hand from the back of her head and let her move her lips from where he had pressed her against his chest.

"Thank you. I can breathe now."

"How are you, baby?" Margaret rushed over and Drake moved aside to allow Elle to be enveloped by her mother.

"I'm fine. Everything is sorted out. How bad is the press?"

Mallory stepped forward and held out a bag. "It was stopped before it could do any real damage. There've been a couple calls, but nothing too pushy. It seems to be contained, but whoever took that photo probably won't like that it's not getting press time. And I brought you clothes and shoes."

"Thank you." Elle looked in the bag and pulled out a wrap dress the same color and shape as her robe, followed by white shoes with a pink stripe across the pointy toe and matching pink and white bow on the toe box.

"I figured if you walked out in this, it's close enough to what you wore this morning to avoid the idea that you were pulled out of bed involuntarily. From a distance, those shoes rather look like bunny slippers. The worst they'll say about you is that you wore white shoes before Memorial Day."

Drake stepped back as Elle reached over to give her friend a hug. "Thank you all so much for staying. It means a lot. Now I just want to get to the office and pretend this never happened."

Drake rubbed his hand over her back as he tried to comfort her. Of course she'd go to work. Elle didn't know how to take a day off. But he'd make sure to spoil her when she got home that night. "Go ahead and get changed while we figure out the logistics."

Elle rose up on her bunny slipper feet and kissed Drake's cheek before heading into the bathroom to change.

"So, can we go now?" Mary asked without whining this time.

Mallory shook her head. "I had to sneak in through the back. There're a couple of reporters out front. I think we should wait here until Elle's gone. When they all leave, we can sneak out the back. Finn, can you bring the car around as if you're just picking her up on a normal day? See if one of the agents can let you borrow a suit coat. They got us into this mess and they can help us get out of it."

"We'll be glad to. Here you go, Finn. I'm about your size." Agent Wallace slipped off his suit jacket and handed it to him. "What else can I do to help, Miss Westin?"

"Mallory, please. And thank you, Agent Wallace. If you hadn't acted so quickly getting that picture down and setting up the groundwork for killing the story, then there'd be more than three photographers out there."

The agent's cheeks blushed as Mallory aimed the full force of her smile at him. "You can call me Damien. Um . . ."

Drake almost felt bad for Agent Wallace. When Mallory poured on the charm, it was hard to think of anything but her. Mallory batted her eyes and Drake thought Damien was going to pass out.

"You were saying, Damien," Mallory mocked as she ran her fingers over her pearls, which only drew attention to her chest. Drake was pretty sure she was flirting. The surprised looks on Bree and Allegra's faces suggested they were thinking the same thing.

"Um. What? Oh, yeah. We can't talk about the case, so please don't ask Miss Simpson about it. But know we are doing what we can to find the person responsible, and Miss Simpson is helping us with that investigation. All of you were a big help and we appreciate it. I'm sorry we had to put you through the questioning, but I'm sure you understand the need for it."

The bathroom door opened and Elle walked out looking somewhat awake. Her face was washed, her hair was pulled back, and bright red lipstick drew attention away from her tired eyes.

"Agent Wallace," Elle said, surprised to see him. "Did I forget to answer something?"

"No, not at all. I was just thanking them for their help and letting them know you can't discuss the case. I also thought to help . . ." He slipped on a Secret Service windbreaker and smiled. "I thought I could escort you outside and thank you profusely in front of the cameras. They'll have to be tricky with their angles since they can't take my picture, but I'll manage it so they get a good picture of the back of me, shaking your hand. Just remember to smile."

"That's really nice of you, thank you. But what about them?" Elle asked of her family.

"We have it all worked out, sweetheart. Just go outside, smile, and shake Damien's hand . . ." Drake started before Elle looked at him funny. "Sorry, you missed introductions between Agent Wallace and Mallory."

"Ah." Elle looked between Mallory and the agent and the light bulb went off in her head.

"Just act as if this was another business meeting. Finn should be outside by now. And I'll see you at home. No working late tonight, okay?" Drake leaned forward and kissed her cheek as she agreed. He knew better than to suggest she take the day off.

"Thank you all. I'll see most of you at the office."

Drake stood back from the window and watched as Damien walked with Elle down the outside stairs and stopped next to Elle's car. Agent Wallace smiled and so did Elle. Damien turned his back to the photographers, held out his hand, and shook Elle's in a friendly way. Elle smiled and even laughed a bit when Damien opened the door for her and waved her off. It only took seconds for the photographers to pull out their cell phones and race to their cars.

Elle sat back in her chair and fought off exhaustion. Jessica had broken out the emergency stash of ice cream and everyone ate in a state of weary shock.

"Well, I thought he was an asshole, but I guess I just needed to bat my eyes." Bree batted her eyes as she made fun of Mallory.

Mallory tossed a small pillow from the couch and hit Bree as she mockingly batted her eyes. "I did not do that."

"Oh yeah you did," the sisters giggled.

"Honey, I could feel a breeze from where I sat with all that batting you were doing. But good luck with that one. Cold fish is my bet. Didn't respond at all when I flirted," Shirley shrugged.

Mallory's bright blue eyes went so wide that Elle almost choked on her chocolate double brownie ice cream.

"I don't see him as a cold fish, but I don't have time to date." Mallory took a bite of her ice cream as if the conversation was over.

"There's always time to date. You have to eat, right?" Bree asked sarcastically.

"Yeah," Allegra smiled mischievously. "And sleep."

"And what do you know about that, young lady?" This time Elle did choke as her mother shot the question right at Allegra.

"You do know that I'm turning thirty this year, right?" Allegra replied with a shake of her head.

"I don't want to know. You're not married and I'm going to leave now, blissfully ignorant of anything else." Margaret gave her daughters each a kiss and headed out.

"Well, I want to know. Spill." Shirley put her finger to her ear to turn up her hearing aid. "Was it one of those fashion models? The ones who fill out those tighty-whities so well?"

"Eww," Mary cringed and got up to leave.

"Yeah, on that note, I'm out." Mallory tossed the empty pint of ice cream and hurried out with Mary.

"What? I want to know, too," Bree said when Elle shook her head.

"I didn't say I was seeing anyone right now. Besides,

I'm not telling." Allegra crossed her arms and Elle knew her sister wasn't going to share any more details.

"Why? I tell you who I'm seeing," Bree complained.

"You haven't seen anyone in almost a year," Elle reminded her.

"Sure, rub it in my face that both my sisters are out dating while I'm slaving away at steel mills and construction sites. Trust me, if you were around those men every day for the past year, you wouldn't want to see anyone either. I'm surprised I can talk without cursing or hitting on one of you."

"Boy, you all are a boring lot. I'm going cruising to find something more interesting to listen to." Shirley rolled out of the office to eavesdrop her way down the hall.

"Well, now that everyone is gone. I wanted to talk to you. I think we need to put one of Mallory's men on Hailey. I saw her flirting with the agents and I don't think they even looked into her. Damien said that they were interrogating her, but it didn't look that way to me." Allegra crossed her arms over her chest and looked seriously at her two sisters.

Elle let out a long breath. She didn't know how she was supposed to keep this from her sisters. She didn't want them running out and doing anything stupid, especially since Elle knew they weren't running in the right direction.

"You know I can't say much, but I will say this. It's not Hailey. They did interrogate her and she has a solid alibi." Elle pulled up her computer and searched the event Hailey had been at. "She was here."

Bree and Allegra leaned forward and looked at the pictures on the screen of her laptop. "Eww. What's she doing there with that old guy?" Allegra asked as she and Bree made a face.

"She was *escorting* him."

Bree and Allegra looked at her, not comprehending her meaning. But then it dawned on Bree. Elle saw her lips twitch and then Bree was giggling. Soon after, Allegra's eyes widened and she joined in the giggling.

"Well, bless her heart. At least it's something she's good at and appears to enjoy," Allegra said as nicely as possible. "But, if it wasn't her, then who was it?"

"You know they don't want me talking about this," Elle reminded her sisters.

"They didn't mean us. We're family after all." Bree shrugged off the confidentiality and plowed straight ahead. "They asked me about Drake. Do they think he's involved?"

Elle refused to say anything. She wasn't going to give any credence to the Secret Service's idea of Drake's involvement.

"So, they do." Bree tapped her finger against her chin as she thought. "It makes sense. He's new to your life, has access to all of your computers, and access to your home where you have your birth certificate, insurance information, social security number—everything you need to steal an identity."

"Yeah, but he couldn't go to the bank or be the person in the picture buying the gun. That person looked a lot like Elle. Except for the shoes."

Elle cocked her head and looked at Allegra. "What shoes?"

"The girl in the picture was wearing ankle straps with her heels. You would never wear those. They're the *it* shoe this season. You know the ones I'm talking about."

Elle shook her head. "No, I don't."

"They're exactly like the pair I gave Mary for her birthday." Allegra paused and looked at her sisters. "Oh my gosh. They're *exactly* like the ones I gave Mary. And Mary looks a lot like you . . ."

"Wait. Is it Cousin Mary or Drake who is behind it? Or both?" Bree slumped back against her chair and shook her head. "I don't believe it, but it kind of makes sense."

"What does?" Elle asked because it didn't make sense to her.

"Cousin Mary. She's always acting as if the world owed her something. And she always brings up money," Bree told them. The sad thing was Elle knew that, too. She just didn't see her actually being gutsy enough to try to steal the money.

"I don't buy that Drake's involved. If it's Mary, she could do the whole thing herself. She works here and no one would think anything of it if she came into your office when you weren't there. She could have easily sent those messages."

"I'm sorry, but no. She's family and she wouldn't do that. Just like Mom said earlier, family sticks together." At least Elle hoped they did.

"I guess Drake could have hired a look-alike. We have to think about it. I mean, we all like him a lot, but he's the newest person to enter your life. And," Bree paused and cringed. "And, after Chord we can't be too careful."

"No. I'm sorry, but Drake is not Chord. And it's not Mary either. It has to be someone else. I just can't imagine . . ." Elle tried not to feel her heart crushing at the thought of Drake or Mary betraying her like this.

"I know, but I don't think you should discount them either. Just be aware of everything. If anything seems off, call one of us. To be honest, I don't like the idea of you being alone with Drake until this is all settled," Bree said while Allegra nodded her agreement.

"I'm done talking about this." Elle could feel her anger rising. It wasn't Drake. And just like the Secret Service, they were going to be looking at the wrong person while the actual criminal was getting away with stealing her identity.

"At least have Mallory upgrade your security. Change the passwords and don't give them to Drake. Just do something different, don't tell anyone, and see what happens."

"Fine, Bree. Now we all need to get back to work." Elle dismissed her sisters and pretended to work as she saw them walk slowly out of the office. They hadn't liked saying those things. Elle knew that, but it didn't mean it didn't bother her that they said them.

Elle pressed the intercom and called Jessica into the office. "I may not be able to control my own life, but I sure as hell can protect my company. Is everything set for my meeting on Monday with Titan?"

"Yes."

"Good. Have all the stock purchases put through today and file the necessary paperwork with the SEC. By tonight, I'll have control of fifty-one percent of their company, and they'll have no idea until I walk into their office Monday morning."

Jessica hurried from the office to make the calls. Elle leaned back in her chair and looked at the financial reports on her screen. This was costing her more money than she wanted, but she had to give the business world a show of power. She hoped that squashing this second takeover attempt would make her point.

Elle saw movement out of her window and jumped. It was just an employee walking down the hall, but she was becoming paranoid. Was it someone who was spying on her? Was it someone who wanted to take Simpson Global from her? Ever since Agent Wallace and Agent Murphy talked to her this morning, she'd been jumping at every shadow, wondering if every person who walked past her was the person trying to destroy her. Elle picked up the phone and called Mallory. She told her of the problems she was having and Bree's suggestion for the security system.

"No problem. I was actually already on my way to play with it. I'll change the password to what you told me and add in some motion detectors. I won't put them in your bedroom, but you have to remember to turn them off before you leave your bedroom or you'll set them off. I should be done in an hour."

"Thank you so much. I think I'll finish up on some of these financial reports and then head home early. It's been too crazy of a night and day for me."

"We'll get to the bottom of this. I'm meeting Damien after I upgrade your security and we're going over everything in my files."

"Damien, huh? When I'm not about to fall over from exhaustion, you'll have to tell me all about it."

"Not too much to tell, but I'll keep you updated."

Mallory hung up and, as Elle put the phone down, she smiled. She was happy for her friend. Mal attracted two types of men. The first group was politicians looking for the perfect power match. But after a date or two with Mallory, they discovered the reason she wasn't close to her parents. She had a fierce independent streak that wouldn't serve well as a politician's wife.

The other group was the police officers she worked with on cases. They were either too intimidated by her family and wealth, or the romance fizzled out as soon as they realized Mallory was not only their equal, but better than most of them when it came to the job. Elle just hoped

Damien didn't fall into that category.

Well, that was enough worrying about Mallory's love life. Elle turned her attention back to the financial documents and started calculating if she was going to need a larger loan to cover the cost of the Bellerose and Titan deals.

Chapter Twenty-Two

Elle opened the door to her condo and the alarm started beeping. She punched in the code and it turned off. Out of habit, she turned it on the "At Home" mode and it instantly went off. The noise startled her so much that she dropped her bag as she jumped.

She let out an exasperated sigh and punched in the code to turn off the alarm as the phone rang. Elle dug through her purse and answered it, assuring the alarm company she was fine as she kicked off Satan's stilettos in different directions. It was then that she saw the note on the kitchen island for her. It was from Mallory letting her know she set up a separate alarm pad in the bedroom.

Elle thought about making an early dinner, but just the mention of her bedroom in the note had her shuffling to her room and closing the door behind her. Elle unbuttoned the dress and let it drop to the floor in front of her chest of drawers. She opened the bottom drawer and found her favorite flannel pants covered with red and pink hearts. Elle dug around further, pulling out a white tank top and putting it on before setting the house alarm and climbing into bed. It may only be four o'clock, but it was time for bed. The pillow felt perfect—the kind of perfect where she wondered if she could live in her bed forever. Elle was almost asleep when the house alarm went off.

The screeching of the alarm caused Elle to jerk up. Her feet tangled in the sheets as she fell from the bed and landed hard on the floor. She froze in place on the floor as the handle to her door turned. The door opened and Elle screamed for her life.

"What? I can't hear you over all this racket," her mother shouted.

Elle opened her eyes and stared at her mother holding her purse in one hand and a small cast iron skillet in the other. "Mom? What are you doing here?"

Elle fumbled with the keypad and turned off the alarm. But before her mother could respond, Elle had to answer the phone and once again swear that she was safe to the security company.

"I brought you something." Margaret held out the small cast iron skillet for Elle.

"Isn't that a little small for cornbread?"

"It's not for cooking. It's for your protection. It's got some heft to it."

"What do you expect me to do with it?"

"Put it in your purse. That way you can clobber someone on the head with it if you need to. You always carry that big bag. That's why I picked up the five-inch skillet—nice and compact. It'll fit perfectly." Her mother shrugged. "I guess it would also make a nice cobbler or maybe a small cookie cake."

Elle placed the heavy skillet on her counter and tried not to roll her eyes. "Fine, now if you don't mind, I'm going back to bed."

Her mother crossed her arms and shook her head. "I'm not leaving until you put it in your purse. I don't want you to forget it."

"Whatever it takes to get you to leave so I can go to

sleep. I don't see how you're still functioning after the day we've had." Elle grabbed the skillet and made her way to where her purse sat on the floor next to a lone stiletto. She opened the bag and shoved the skillet in, not caring if she broke anything inside. She'd do just about anything to get her mom out of her place so she could get to sleep.

"See, that wasn't so hard, was it?" Her mom wrapped her up in a hug and kissed her forehead. "I just want you to be safe. Should I stay? I could put off going to the Children's Hospital if my baby needs me."

"I know you want to keep me safe, Mom. That's why I'll carry the stupid thing. I can't wait to see the reaction when I have to go through security somewhere with that in my purse." Elle hugged her back. "And no, I don't need you to stay. In fact, I think you should go home. We all need our sleep and then you can actually stay awake for story time at the hospital."

Margaret waved her off. "I'm perfectly fine. I'm just going for a bit, and then I'll head home. I'll call later to check on you."

"How about tomorrow? I fully plan on turning my ringer off and not leaving that bed until morning."

"Fine, but I'll still call tonight. If you're awake, you can answer." Her mother wrapped her up in a final hug and kissed her cheek. "Call me if you need anything. I love you."

"Love you, too." Elle waited until her mother left and then shuffled back to her room and reset the alarm. She picked her sheets up from the floor and was arranging the bed when the shrill of the alarm erupted again.

"Mom, stop coming in without knocking," Elle screamed as she turned off the alarm once again and went to answer the ringing phone. "Mom?"

Elle answered the phone. "Are you okay, Miss Simpson?" the man from the control center asked.

"I thought it was my mom, but she's not saying anything. I don't hear anyone out there."

"I'll send the police."

"No! I'm sure it's just another false alarm. I'm going to check." Elle reached for the door handle.

"Keep me on the line. The police are just a button-push away."

Elle nodded in response and then felt silly for nodding to a man over the phone. Taking a deep breath, Elle tried to steady her shaking hands as she reached for the doorknob. Maybe hiding under the bed until the police came wasn't such a bad idea after all.

"Are you still there, Miss Simpson? What set off the alarm?"

"I'm almost there. Hold on." Elle closed her eyes, took another deep breath, and pressed her ear to the door. When she didn't hear any strange noises, she finally opened the door.

Her eyes darted around her home, taking in every nook and cranny where a bad person could hide. When had her curtain looked so malicious? And she was going to have to replace that picture of her grandmother on the wall. It was way too creepy in the shadows of the room. It had made her think someone was standing there watching her.

Elle moved her eyes to the front door and saw a stack of menus lying on the floor. She let out a sigh of relief along with a chuckle. "Menus for the takeout places nearby. I guess the alarm went off when they slid them under the door. My mom must have let someone into the building when she left. Sadly, she does that all the time. She's single-handedly responsible for a 400-percent rise in Chinese delivery to my building. I'm sorry to have bothered you with this—again."

"No problem. That's what we're here for. Have a good afternoon, Miss Simpson."

Elle picked up the menus and tossed them onto the table. That was it; no more alarm waking her up. She turned it to Silent and turned off her phone. She was going to bed once and for all.

Elle rolled over and reached out for Drake. She'd been dreaming of him but instead of feeling his warm, hard body, she felt the empty pillow. Strange, she thought for sure she'd been asleep far longer than just an hour. She nuzzled back into her pillow but froze when she heard a sound.

It was so quiet that Elle almost went back to sleep. But when she closed her eyes, she heard it again. It sounded like the slight scuff of a shoe on the hardwood floor. "Drake?"

Elle sat up in bed and listened again. Pots banged and the cabinet door slammed closed. A second later the water in the sink came on. Instantly her heart rate lowered. Elle pushed the covers back and swung her legs out of bed. Slipping her feet into her bunny slippers, she left the warmth of her bed to see if she could talk Drake into coming to bed early.

"Hey, honey. I didn't know you were coming over tonight," Elle called out as she pushed open the door. She saw the pot in the sink with the water overflowing its sides. The hair on her arms stood up as she froze in place. The sound of a foot scuffing the floor to her side had her whipping her head around and coming face-to-face with a tall man in a black ski mask.

Elle reacted instantly. Her fist connected with his face

just as Finn and Tigo had taught her. She pulled her arm back for another punch, but it was too late. She felt something connect with the back of her head, and then Elle saw nothing but stars as she fell to the ground.

The world slowly came into focus as a man's voice brought her out of the darkness. He wasn't talking to her, though. Instead he was cursing at something or someone. Elle's heart rate spiked—she knew that voice. It couldn't be him. She peeked out from under her lashes and had to work hard to prevent the gasp when she saw him working on her laptop. But it wasn't him that caused her head to swim and her heart to pound against her chest so hard Elle feared she might die. No, it was the woman with him. The betrayal cut so deep Elle must have made a noise because that face so familiar to her turned and looked at her.

"You were only out for three minutes. Guess I didn't hit you hard enough."

"How could you?" Elle struggled to ask as her head swam.

"Power. Love. Fame. Pick one."

Elle didn't have a chance to ask any more questions. The stun gun was pressed to her neck, and the world went dark once again.

Chapter Twenty-Three

D rake sat at his desk and filled Phillip in on all the details from the past twenty-four hours. Phillip clutched his stomach and tried not to fall out of his chair as Drake told him about the Secret Service busting down the bedroom door and hauling him out of bed completely naked. Soon he was regretting telling his best friend the story. He was never going to live it down.

By the time Phillip left the office, Drake was thinking he needed a new best friend. By telling the events of the day, he stopped caring about the long hours of interrogation he had been through. All he could think of was how much he loved Elle and how he didn't want to spend any more time apart. Sure, relationships take work and he was ready for anything the world put them up against. With her by his side, they would face it and conquer it together.

He opened his desk and pulled out the velvet box to look at the ring inside. This weekend was it. He felt energy surging through his body, urging him to hurry. He was going to spoil Elle tonight with so much love that when he asked her to marry him, she'd say "yes" for sure. But first he needed to go to the store and pick up something amazing to make for dinner. Then he'd stop at the florist and finally sneak into Elle's condo. If he moved fast enough, he could get to her place and get the perfect night of romance all set up before she got home from work.

Drake balanced the groceries on his hip as he dug through his pocket for the key to Elle's condo. He slid the key into the lock and opened the door. He kicked the pile of take-out menus on the floor out of the way and shut the door.

The groceries fell from his arm when he looked into the living room. Elle lay unconscious on the floor, and two people dressed in black were sitting at her desk. They turned at the sound of the groceries dropping, and they all stared at each other, no one daring to move. The intruders were waiting to see what Drake was going to do, and Drake was glancing around to decide his best plan of action.

He could run out the door and get help, but there was no way he was leaving Elle. Instead anger boiled his blood, and he had to clench his fists to keep from launching himself blindly toward them. He didn't know the woman, but he sure as hell knew the man typing something on Elle's computer.

"I would say it's nice to see you again, but we both know that's a lie." Drake took a casual step forward.

"Likewise."

"Is Elle hurt?"

"Not too badly. But as soon as I send these emails she will be. Such a shame when someone commits suicide. They tend to spill their guts, literally and figuratively. Poor Elle is going to hang herself for all the evil things she did as outlined in this email I'm sending to her whole contact list. The fraud, the embezzlement, the money laundering, the SEC violations — she just couldn't live with herself any longer. I guess now it'll have to be a murder-suicide. In the long run, that's even better. Then when the stock tanks at Monday morning's bell, I'm going to buy the whole company for a quarter of what it's worth. I'll make a killing. Get it?"

Drake tried to think rationally, but his baser instincts kicked in. Unable to stop himself, he shoved the woman out of the way. She stumbled back, tripping over Elle, and fell out of sight into the bedroom. Chord McAlister leaped from the chair, sending it smashing to the floor. Drake closed his fist and connected with Chord's stomach. Air whooshed from him as Drake landed another punch. Chord then grabbed his shoulders and slammed him against the wall. The wall shook and picture frames crashed to the ground.

Elle heard a crash but couldn't open her eyes. The floor shook as she focused all her power on moving her fingers. Feelings started to work their way back through her body. When she opened her eyes, it took some blinking to bring the world into focus. When her vision cleared, Elle had trouble believing what she saw. Drake and Chord were fighting in her living room. Her coffee table shattered as Drake sent Chord careening into it with a well-placed punch to the face, but it was the sight of Becca, her friend, sorority sister, and former roommate, sneaking forward with her taser that got Elle moving.

With a quick glance around her condo, the only thing Elle could reach was one of Satan's stilettos. The white and pink stiletto she'd kicked off earlier sat three feet from her. Elle grabbed the shoe and gripped it so tightly her fingers turned white. Becca stood with her long hair pulled into a ponytail, her mask forgotten in the back pocket of her black skinny jeans.

Elle slowly moved to a crouch. Becca's back was to her as she stood near where Drake and Chord were locked in their fight. She was waiting for a clear shot to zap Drake, and Elle wasn't about to give it to her. With a grunt, Elle pushed off and lunged at Becca. She raised her arm high and brought Satan's stiletto down onto Becca's shoulder as hard as she could.

Becca dropped the taser as she screeched in pain. The heel had gone straight into the bare skin next to her neck and was now embedded there. She turned around and stared at Elle with wild eyes. The men stopped and stared as Becca wrenched the stiletto from her shoulder and screamed at Elle.

"I have felt so guilty for years because of you. You were perfect. Working hard, studying constantly, having men fawn over your girl-next-door looks. But it never mattered to you. You took it for granted that everyone loved you and all these wonderful things just kept falling in your lap. Chord, your company . . ."

Elle backed up to the front door as Becca stalked toward her. Chord took advantage of the distraction and leapt on Drake, causing him to stumble backward.

"Becca, did you think I wanted my company like this? My father died. I would have given it back in a heartbeat if that meant I had him back. You knew how devastated I was. We were roommates. You know how a piece of me never recovered from losing him." Elle's heel hit something hard and she looked down to see her purse. The cast iron skillet sat inside, the handle sticking out like a beacon.

"Oh, I know how you used it to your advantage after I gave you my shoulder to cry on. Chord told me how you used the death of your father to close deals and win over shareholders by making them feel sorry for you. Thank goodness I didn't let your holier-than-thou act stop me from sleeping with him when you were dating. That's the only good thing you did for me—bring him into my life." Becca clutched the bloodied heel in her hand and took another step forward.

The betrayal of her friend made Elle sick. "You were sleeping with Chord when we were dating? How could you? You were my friend, Becca."

"Some friend you were. As you rose in power and importance, did you bring me along with you? No, then you sent Chord away, and I was alone for years. You took those years from us and now you're going to pay for it."

Becca pulled her arm back with the stiletto in hand. Elle bent to the side and made a grab for her purse. Her hands tightened on the rough cast iron handle. Elle swung with all her strength as Becca moved in for the strike. Her purse flew off as the skillet arched through the air. Becca's eye's widened in surprise as she hurriedly stabbed at Elle.

The skillet landed with a hard *thud* against Becca's head, sending shockwaves rippling up Elle's arms. Becca dropped the stiletto an inch from where it would have struck Elle on the top of her head. The shoe bounced off her shoulder as Becca's eyes rolled back in her head, and she crumpled to the floor.

Elle's breathing was heavy as she fought against the blackness trying to close in on her vision. Slowly, she leaned down and pressed two fingers against her old friend's neck. Elle let out a sigh of relief when she felt a pulse. An angry bump on Becca's head was already starting to form. But it was the sound of glass breaking that had Elle looking away from Becca. Drake had been slammed against the mirror in the living room and Chord had his hands wrapped around Drake's throat.

Drake fought for breath as Chord's fingers tightened. A trickle of blood ran into Drake's eye, but he could still see the twisted smile on Chord's lips. He was enjoying slowly taking Drake's life.

Drake struggled against the hold. He tried to pry Chord's fingers loose, but Chord just tightened them further. Drake kicked out and connected with Chord's leg, but he lacked the strength to do any damage. Then he saw Elle. Her golden hair was wild as she crept forward. Drake had to blink the blood out of his eye. He thought he was hallucinating; it looked as though she had a skillet raised above her head. Somehow, he had to protect Elle. He couldn't leave her to face Chord alone.

He struck out his leg again, this time managing to hit Chord on the inner thigh. Reflexively, Chord loosened his hold and stepped back. Drake dragged in all the air he could before the fingers tightened around his neck again. His vision cleared as the door shattered in, and Elle hammered the skillet down on Chord's head.

"Secret Service!"

"Police!"

Chord staggered back and turned slightly toward Elle. Drake saw the evil glint in his eye before Chord stumbled toward her. Chord reached for Elle as Agent Wallace and Drake lunged forward. Elle pulled back her arms and swung.

A resounding *thud* filled the room as Elle smashed the skillet into Chord's smirking face. Drake landed on top of Chord, who collapsed to the ground. The wind was knocked out of Drake a split second later when Agent Wallace landed hard on him. Drake lay stunned and gasping for breath while Agent Wallace stood up. Police officers helped Drake to his feet.

Drake saw Elle, chest heaving, trying to control her breathing as she clung to the cast iron skillet still clutched in her hand. She was breathtaking with her hair hanging over her shoulders. Her white tank top clung to her curves while one ear of her bunny slipper dangled on the ground.

The agents were talking, but Drake didn't hear them. Elle's eyes were locked with his and the rest of the room fell away. Neither seemed to notice Becca hurling insults as she was being handcuffed and taken away. Drake stepped around Chord's unconscious body and the agents surrounding him. He ignored Agent Wallace's questions and stopped before Elle. He reached out and ran his hand down her bare arm. His fingers closed over the handle of the skillet and he gently tugged it from her grasp.

"I don't want you to hit me with this if I say something wrong." Blindly he dropped the skillet to the floor by his feet. Drake reached for her hands and lifted them to his lips for a gentle kiss.

"I had it all planned. Dinner, bubble bath, romance . . ." Drake started. He should have been nervous, but he wasn't. He'd known it from the first time their fingers touched at the ball. Elle was his and he was hers.

Drake dropped her right hand and knelt before her. He kept her left hand in between his hands as he looked up at her. "You deserve better than this, but I'm a selfish man. I can't stand the thought of being separated from you for one more day. You are my sun, moon, and stars. I look forward to rising every morning with you and going to bed with you every night. You enflame my passion for life to the point I think anything is possible as long as you're by my side."

Drake dug into his pocket and pulled out the velvet box. The top had been smashed and was now askew, but the ring still nestled inside it. He pried open the top and held out the ring. "Elle, I want to spend the rest of my life with your bunny slippers beside our bed, discarded heels strewn about the house, and emergency stashes of ice cream in the freezer. Will you marry me?"

Elle moved her eyes from the ring Drake was clutching between his fingers to his face. There was a cut above his eye and one on his cheek. His shirt wasn't tucked in and some of the buttons were missing. He'd never been more handsome to her than he was at that moment.

Her heart melted as he flashed her a smile filled with such happiness that it had Elle laughing. "Yes. Yes, I'll marry you."

She held out her hand and Drake slipped the ring onto her finger. It was then Elle heard the clapping and whistles. Police officers and Secret Service agents filled the room. She even saw Mallory standing near the door whistling loudly. But when Drake rose to his feet and wrapped his arms around her, she stopped thinking about the others in the room. In fact, Elle was pretty sure no one else existed in the whole world when his lips touched hers. Colors, sounds, and even Chord lying on the floor melted away as his tongue lovingly stroked hers. Drake's hands held her anchored against him as her heart soared to the stars and beyond.

Chapter Twenty-Four

The smell of dinner made his mouth water. He sat on the couch in his future mother-in-law's house and laughed at the two mothers in the kitchen planning the wedding and picking out what they wanted to be called by their grandchildren.

Yesterday had been a blur. After Chord and Becca had been carted off to the hospital, the police and Secret Service had intruded on their engagement. They'd answered questions for hours until Mallory casually mentioned to Agent Wallace that he had everything he needed and now may be a good time to let the happy couple celebrate. And celebrate they did.

Unfortunately, the wolves would not stay at bay long. At eight this morning, the alarm in Elle's apartment went off. Unlike the silent alarm Chord and Becca triggered when they entered, this one had Drake and Elle shooting out of bed as the siren sounded. He'd grabbed the cast iron skillet that was sitting on the nightstand and almost conked Margaret on the head. She'd been so thrilled about the engagement that she didn't even notice he was naked until Elle wrapped her robe around his waist.

From what Drake could get from Margaret's excited chatter, Mallory had told Bree this morning and then Bree quickly spread the word. Reid was even flying home to celebrate. Margaret had declared she would host an engagement dinner. Knowing when to give up, he'd called his parents and sent his private jet to Florida to get them.

Now he had Elle leaning against his side with his arm around her as Mallory told the story of her getting the call from the security company and coming right in time to see Becca dragged out of the condo and Drake propose.

"It was so romantic," she said with a big smile on her face.

"See, Elle, a mother knows these things. I told you that skillet would come in handy." Margaret held up her own large skillet full of peach cobbler.

"I'll never doubt you again, Mom," Elle swore.

"But how did Chord and Becca pull it off? I still don't understand how they were able to get into your computer." Bree crossed her legs and waited for answers.

"It's all my fault," Elle said sadly.

"How could it be your fault?" Allegra wondered.

"I was too trusting. Agent Wallace told me that roommates and ex-boyfriends are some of the most likely identity thieves. They have complete access to your life. They know my first pet's name and my mother's maiden name. They have my phone number, birthday, address, and can easily look in my purse for my driver's license number. Chord had used my computer numerous times when we were together. He knew the passwords I used. Foolishly, I hadn't changed any of them. I was too worried I'd forget them. All it took was trying a couple of my old passwords and he was able to hack into my email.

"Then Becca sat in our lobby, just like we thought Hailey had, and tried to get online. When she couldn't, she talked one of the employees into giving her the Wi-Fi password. We don't know which employee yet. She used the password Chord had discovered and sent the press release from my email."

Drake gave her shoulder a reassuring squeeze. "When Elle's excellent press conference only made her more popular, they moved on to identity theft. Too bad for them they got busted on that as well. When they didn't get the money, Chord came up with the idea of emailing the White House. Becca bought the gun in Elle's name."

"I can't believe Becca did this. She used to be so nice. She'd let me borrow clothes and we'd go out to clubs while you were studying," Bree said in disbelief.

Elle understood. She was still in shock, too. But as the shock wore off, the pain of what her friend did to her was starting to turn to anger. In time, it would turn to pity. "Well, Damien called me and told me they were turning on each other before they even got into the interview room. At least it looks like there won't have to be a trial. I'm just glad we can move past it and start focusing on the future."

"A future with a wedding dress," Margaret called from the kitchen.

"And grandchildren," Drake's mom added as everyone in the living room laughed.

"Well, it's about time I head out." Mallory leaned down and gave Elle a hug. "Congratulations to you both. And I expect a beautiful bridesmaid dress, not some hideous southern belle hoop skirt contraption."

"Damn. I had it all picked out. Everyone would be in pastels with matching parasols." Elle laughed as Mallory and her sisters cringed. "Can't you stay? Reid should be here soon. You haven't seen him since high school. You're always rushing off before he comes over."

Mallory's face tightened and she pasted on her debutante smile. "Sorry, I've got a date with Damien."

Elle watched and wondered why those two refused to be in the same room together. It wasn't just Mallory. It was Reid, too. Whenever Elle asked them if anything was wrong, they'd just say "nothing" with fake smiles on their faces. Something had to have happened between them, but for the life of her she couldn't get either of them to tell her.

"Well, have fun on your date. Can't wait to hear all about it on Monday." Elle gave her best friend a wink to let her know she wasn't going to push the Reid topic. But that didn't mean she wouldn't ask Reid while he was here.

"Definitely. And I'll be waiting to hear how your takeover goes. I wish I could see their faces. I wonder if they've found out about Chord's arrest?" Mallory asked as she slid into her coat.

"I don't think so. It's the weekend so there are no arraignment or bail hearings. Plus the Secret Service is still interviewing them to determine their threat level against the President. Agent Wallace told me that local authorities are also talking to them about guilty pleas for the other charges, like our attempted murder." Drake gave her shoulder another squeeze, and she decided she was done talking about it. She had happier things to discuss.

As Mallory headed out the door, Mary made her way in. Drake stood and said hello before going to sit with his dad for a moment. The sisters took a collective deep breath and let it out before turning to smile at Mary.

"I'm sorry I gave you so much work to do today. I hope you don't mind." Elle had decided to pass off all the media inquiries that were trickling in to Mary. She had wanted more responsibility, and with Elle's desire to get Jessica more involved in the financial side, it made sense to give Mary a shot at handling all of the press.

"It's not the work, it's the worry," Mary said on a sigh.

"I hope I did a good job. We got a couple calls after you left the Secret Service office yesterday."

"I'm sure you did just fine." Elle took a second to look Mary over. She didn't look like her normal frumpy self. "You look beautiful, Mary."

"I was just about to say the same thing. Did you get those clothes from my rack room?" Allegra asked. She had a whole room in the building reserved for clothes any executive could borrow for press conferences, shows, conventions, and such.

Mary blushed. "I did. I thought it was open to everyone."

"It is, and you look fantastic. We need to go shopping and get you a whole new wardrobe. We could start at this cute little boutique on Peachtree . . ." Allegra started before stopping at Mary's look.

"You'd go shopping with me?" Mary asked with wonder.

"Of course, it's what cousins do. We shop, we share clothes, have drinks together, and talk about men." Allegra grinned.

"Thank you. I'd like that. I had to have someone help me pick this out, so it would be great if I had your fashion sense helping me."

"Who helped — ?" Allegra started, but was cut off.

"Oh, it's six o'clock. Turn on the news," Mary cried as she wrung her hands.

The sisters looked at each other. Bree shrugged and picked up the remote, turning the television on. Two serious reporters sat behind a desk with a picture of Elle smiling as she shook hands with Agent Wallace filling the corner of the screen. Damien's back was to them, but it was clear there were no hard feelings between them.

"Local business tycoon Elle Simpson, CEO of Simpson Global, is in the news today for something besides business. There had been reports that Miss Simpson had been taken from her home at two o'clock in the morning wearing nothing but her pajamas, bunny slippers, and a pair of handcuffs," the overly tan male anchor said into the camera as the picture of Elle and Damien went to full screen.

The woman anchor gave a serious nod before picking up the story. "The Secret Service talked to us only to say that Miss Simpson was helping with an investigation. They stated that she was nice enough to spare her time in the middle of the night in order to offer her support. It's clear from this photo that Miss Simpson was not in her pajamas or handcuffed when she left their office yesterday afternoon. We talked with Mary Hines, head of public relations for Simpson Global, this afternoon and here is what she had to say."

Mary filled the screen as she sat in a chair in her office. Her hair fell in soft waves around her shoulders and her makeup was flawless. The jade dress accented her coloring and showed off curves Elle didn't know her cousin had. The video clip started and Mary smiled sweetly into the camera.

"What do Miss Simpson and Simpson Global have to say about the report stating Miss Simpson was arrested by the Secret Service early yesterday morning and the subsequent comment from the Secret Service about her assisting them on a case?" a reporter asked from off-screen.

"At no time was Miss Simpson under arrest." Mary waved off as if it was the most absurd comment she'd ever heard. "Miss Simpson has had the satisfaction of assisting the Secret Service with an undisclosed matter. Unfortunately, we cannot say more at this time. It is up to the Secret Service to give the details of the case, but I understand in most cases they do not. However, we at Simpson Global would like to thank them and all public servants for the hard work they do in keeping our country and its citizens safe. Thank you."

The video cut away and the woman anchor nodded. "Our studio would like to thank them as well. We do not usually hear much from the Secret Service. They are, of course, most known for protecting the President of the United States."

"That's right, Tandy. We don't want to speculate, but it appears Miss Simpson helped them carry out their job over the weekend. We shouldn't be surprised. Miss Simpson, along with her boyfriend, Drake Charles, is known in the community for her generous contributions to the Children's Hospital."

The whole room turned and silently looked at Mary as the anchors tossed it to weather. Mary gripped her hands in front of her as she looked nervously around the room.

"Was it that bad?" Mary asked finally.

"Bad? It was excellent! That's it. You're in charge of every interview from now on," Elle declared as she got up and hugged Mary. "I'm so proud of you."

The front door banged open and Reid, in all of his playboy glory, dropped his bag and looked around. "I'm here. The party can start now. But first, as the man of the family, I need to have a few words with the fiancé."

Elle rolled her eyes and knew her sisters were doing the same thing. As much as she loved her elusive brother, he was last person to try to take an authoritative role in the family. But when Reid wrapped her in a bear hug, all she cared about was that her brother was finally home. What he really needed was a good woman to settle him down. Gosh, now she felt just like her mother.

"Oh, please. More like the boy of the family," Bree teased as Elle moved out of the way so she could hug him, too.

"Thank goodness our new brother will be in town more than a couple times a year to take care of us helpless damsels in distress." Allegra smacked Reid's shoulder before jumping up into his arms. "I'm so glad you came. I missed you."

"I missed you all, too. Who knows, maybe my next project will be stateside."

"That would be fantastic! All my babies here with me . . . what more could a mother want?" Elle watched her mom pinch Reid's cheek and smile lovingly up at him. "Except to see all my babies happily married. Of course some grandchildren wouldn't hurt, either."

"Mom," they all whined as Margaret headed back into the kitchen complaining about the hours of labor she went through and that it wasn't like she was asking for much. Her friend Judy had three grandchildren already. The siblings all looked at each other and broke out in laughter.

Drake sat back enjoying the taste of the peach cobbler lingering on his lips. Elle sat next to him, telling the table a story from their childhood while resting her small hand on his leg. If this was what life was going to be like from now on, then he'd finally become rich.

"Mom, if you don't mind, I wanted to talk to the men here about business real quick. Dinner was wonderful." Elle smiled at her mom.

Drake hid his surprise, but Reid didn't. From what he knew about Reid's side of the company, Elle rarely ventured over there. And he didn't know what he had to do with Simpson Global business. "Me, too?"

"You, too. Come on, boys." Elle slid her chair back and headed for the back patio. Drake looked at his future brother and they both shrugged.

Drake followed Reid out onto the patio and took a seat next to Reid. He suddenly felt as if he were in the principal's office as Elle took the seat across from them and clasped her hands together.

"So, what'd we do?" Reid asked with one side of his mouth quirked up, clearly enjoying this.

"It's not what you've done, but what you're going to do."

"I'm not going dress shopping and I won't be your man of honor." Elle gave her brother a look and Reid just laughed it off.

"Drake, you've been talking about wanting to expand DCE away from smartphones. Have you ever thought of integrated-touch screen systems for hotels?"

"I've had some ideas but don't have a test subject. Now that we're done with our huge project for the government, I can look into it. Why?"

"Yeah, why?" Reid asked.

"You said you wouldn't mind coming home, right?" Elle saw him nod hesitantly before continuing. "Well, as a nice bonus to my acquisition of Titan Industries on Monday, Simpson Global will become the proud owner of 250 acres of property right outside of Atlanta. Sitting on it is an almost complete luxury resort, pool area, convention center, stables, shooting range, lake, and spa." Elle sat back, crossed her arms, and grinned as she watched the men soak it in.

"How much is 'almost complete'?" Reid asked.

"Pool area, stables, spa, and convention center are

complete with the exception of furniture, paint, and other last-minute things. Structure for the hotel is complete. Electrical wiring and plumbing are complete as well. Interior design needs work, including electronics like televisions and, optimally, a fully integrated system from DCE. Drake, if you're interested, I want you to go wild. Everything designed around the comfort of the guests. In-room touch screens to set temperature, order room service, select television stations, make reservations at local restaurants or clubs—anything they need just a simple touch away."

"Wild, huh? I'm in. My lab is going to be so excited. This is a lot more fun than government contracts."

Reid pinched his lips together in thought. "Do we have the funds to complete it?"

"We will when we sell off some of Titan's less prominent holdings. I think we can free up a good amount of capital. Plus there's a couple other international investors who are covering twenty-five percent of the total cost."

"I'll supply the technology in exchange for one percent ownership in the hotel," Drake put in. "I've been wanting to expand my holdings. Of course, I'll retain the patents, though."

"Sounds good to me," Reid said, nodding. "And you're wanting me to take over completion to get the resort up and running?"

"That and one more thing. We have the space; I think we should build an arena on the far side of the property. We can even put in a private airstrip if we want. We could hold concerts, sporting events, and conventions. I want you to research that and see if we could get some contracts for appearances if we build it. See what can make it different from everywhere else."

"I can do that. I need a month or so to finish up in Europe, but then I can get to work on it full time. That's a real nice added bonus. And you say Titan has no idea this takeover is coming?"

"None. I bought all the shares officially on Friday at four in the afternoon. The reports were filed, but they won't go out until next week. I'm going in on Monday to let them know."

"Can I come with you? I'd like to get all the plans immediately."

"Wait, my brother at a business meeting? Not just a business meeting, but a serious and probably tense board meeting? Oh, do you feel that?" Elle asked sarcastically as she rubbed her arms.

"Feel what?" Reid asked hesitantly as Drake watched the siblings with amusement.

"That cold air from hell freezing over."

Reid shook his head and Elle giggled. He stood up and held out his hand to Drake. "I'm looking forward to working with you on this."

Drake shook his hand. After Reid went inside, he motioned for Elle to come sit on his lap. "Thanks for including me on this. We've been looking for something fun to sink our teeth into. It'll also give me more of a reason to come to your office."

He felt her breasts pressing against his chest as she leaned forward, wrapping her arms around his neck. "I can think of plenty of reasons for you to come to my office," she whispered into his ear.

Drake grinned and slipped his hand under her skirt. "I don't think I'll have any trouble with that. Let's get home. I'm ready to celebrate again."

Elle screamed out Drake's name as he pushed her over the edge. Her body tightened around him as waves of pleasure pulsed through her body. His eyes never left hers as he thrust into her over and over. He moved harder and faster as he braced his arms at her sides, drawing out her cries. She grabbed his arms, flexed with tension, and held on as he lost himself in her.

His pace faltered as he grew near his finish. Gone was the elegance of lovemaking. All that was left were their moans filling the room as they battled each other for pleasure. Elle bit her lip as the tension began to build again and raced toward it as she met him thrust for thrust. She dug her nails into his shoulder as he flexed into her. When Drake bent his head and pulled her nipple into his mouth, she felt the tension break over her and this time brought him with her.

Drake collapsed onto her before rolling off to the side and tucking her against his chest. She ran her fingers across his chest as they lay quietly, trying to catch their breath.

Elle snuggled closer to him. "I love you, Drake."

"I love you too, sweetheart. I have a request, though?"

"What is it?"

"Can we celebrate our engagement like this every night for the rest of our lives?"

Elle laughed and smacked his arm. "Every night, huh?"

Drake pulled her on top of him with a devilish smile. "Let me convince you why it's a good idea."

And he did.

Chapter Twenty-Five

"You can't go in there, miss! Sir, please, you can't go in there," the Titan Industries secretary called as she chased Elle and Reid down the hall.

Elle smiled at the young woman and flashed a copy of the documentation showing her ownership of fifty-one percent of the company. "Yes I can. I now own the majority of Titan Industries. I'm Elle Simpson and it's nice to meet you. Now, please excuse me while I break the news to your boss. Unless you want to do that?"

The woman stepped back and shook her head. "Mr. Eldrich is not going to like this."

"Probably not." Reid flashed her a killer smile and held out his hand. "Hi, I'm Reid Simpson, and you are…?"

Elle elbowed her brother. "For crying out loud, Reid. We're here to take over the company, not to flirt. Thank goodness you're going back to Europe tonight. Now, please excuse us."

"I'm sorry, but am I about to lose my job?"

Elle turned to face the woman who was around Allegra's age. She had a small diamond ring on her finger and the beginning of a baby bump. Elle could see why she'd be so worried. "What's your name?"

"Emily Foxworth."

"Emily, what do you do here? I mean, really. Not the job you were hired for, but the job you actually do."

"I'm Mr. Eldrich's personal assistant." She paused and looked up at the ceiling before looking into Elle's eyes. "Honestly?"

"Honestly."

"I do everything. He's always with his cronies golfing or drinking at the club. He tosses grand ideas at me and considers that running the company as I'm left to figure out what he meant and how to get it done. I pick up his dry cleaning, gifts for his friends and family, plan the company's and his family's Christmas party, get him coffee, write all his speeches, answer all his correspondence, give him a summary of what I said to whom at the end of the week, and handle his personal finances so he doesn't blow through his fortune."

Elle nodded her head. Not all CEOs were like this. She had worked with some great ones, but anyone who would hire Chord couldn't be one of the good guys. "When things start moving here, I want you to call to schedule a conference with me so that you can fill me in on all the details of the company. The who's who and the what's what. If what you say checks out, then no, you won't be fired. Instead, you'll likely be promoted. However, you need to take risks and speak up if you want to move up the corporate ladder."

"I bet you also have the details on the resort Titan is building outside of town, don't you?" Reid asked with an easy smile.

"Thank you for the advice, Miss Simpson. I guess no one is going to move the glass ceiling for us. We simply have to bust through it. And, yes, Mr. Simpson, I have all of that information. Do you need it?"

"I would love to have the original of everything you have, if you don't mind. You can keep a copy here in the office. Thank you, Emily." Reid gave her a wink and Elle gave Emily her card.

"Now, I take it the meeting is this way?" Elle pointed to the large decorative wood door at the end of the hall.

"Yes. Good luck, Miss Simpson." Elle smiled and strode down the hall as she heard Emily whisper, "You'll need it."

The smell of cigar smoke reached her first. Loud guffaws came next. As Elle approached the door, she heard the roomful of men. Reid put his hands in his pockets and rocked back on his heels.

"Sounds like my kind of party."

"Why did I bring you?" Elle shook her head and took a deep breath. It was time to follow the advice she'd just given Emily.

She may have been handed her company, but that didn't mean glass ceilings weren't in her way. At first, she'd been timid and quiet. She expected the other executives to see the hard work she was doing and appreciate it. But the business world doesn't work like that. So she straightened her back and demanded respect by playing the game better than the men did. As Elle stared at the door, she felt secure that she was playing the game and winning. Not only that, she was changing the rules.

"I wonder where Chord is? The meeting started ten minutes ago."

"Only one thing to make a man late."

Elle listened to the peals of laughter as they talked and could picture them winking at each other.

"It doesn't matter. That little lady is way out of her league. I'm surprised Simpson Global hasn't been taken over before. It sure is a sweet piece of ass — the company and its CEO."

Elle felt Reid stiffen behind her. "I'm going to punch . . ."

"Don't worry about it. It happens all the time."

"It does?" Reid cursed under his breath and put his hand on her shoulder. Suddenly she felt as if they were back in the principal's office trying to gain entry to Windsor Academy. She spoke up then and she was going to do it now.

Elle tossed a grin over her shoulder to Reid. "This is going to be fun."

She pushed open the door and strode into the room as if she owned it. And for all intents and purposes, she did. "Thank you, gentlemen. I think my ass is pretty nice, too." Elle gave them a look of pity as she shrugged her shoulders. "Unfortunately, you'll never get to see under mine or my company's skirt to find out. But good try."

A man in his mid-sixties with a ruddy face whom she recognized as Mr. Eldrich took a long drag on his cigar and blew the smoke into her face. "I'm sorry to disagree with you, Miss Simpson. But after today, I can do whatever I want to that pretty ass of yours. See, I've been buying up shares of Simpson Global and have called an emergency shareholder meeting this afternoon. You'll be voted out and I'll be voted in."

Reid stepped forward, but Elle gently touched the sleeve of his suit to let him know she could handle it. "I'm sorry but that meeting no longer exists as of last night."

Mr. Eldrich's face darkened a deeper shade of red. It was obvious he wasn't used to anyone challenging him. "When Chord McAlister gets here, he'll show you the paperwork that Titan Industries owns over twenty-five percent of Simpson Global. It'll be easy to get the rest of the shareholders to vote you out. There are only two other major shareholders, and I'm sure I can convince the rest of those small, insignificant trusts and know-nothing day traders to side with me."

"I hate to be the bearer of bad news, but Chord won't be making it today. He's unavailable for the next," she turned and looked at Reid, "twenty years?"

"I'd say thirty or forty, but what's a decade or two?" Reid laughed to the un-amused faces around the large table.

"What are you talking about?" Mr. Eldrich demanded.

"Only that he's in the custody of the government for identity theft, bank fraud, threats made against the President of the United States, assault, battery, and, oh yeah, attempted murder. Now, I have some papers to show you gentlemen."

Elle slowly walked around the table handing out copies of her filings with the SEC. "These are my proof of ownership of fifty-one percent of the company—*your* company. Furthermore, I have assurances from another ten percent of shareholders that they will vote with me in favor of merging Titan Industries into Simpson Global."

"But . . ."

"I thought we already discussed there are no buts for you—pun fully intended. See, Mr. Eldrich, this sweet piece of ass knows a thing or two about business." The knock on the door stopped Elle as Emily pushed open the door and handed a full box of material to Reid. "Thank you, Emily."

"What do you think you're doing, girl?" Mr. Eldrich bellowed.

Emily squared her shoulders and faced him. "I'm giving all the resort documentation to my new boss. Good-bye, Mr. Eldrich. I'll start packing your office for you."

Emily walked out the door and Elle couldn't help but smile as Eldrich and the rest of the men around the table sputtered with indignation. "As I was saying, I know a bit about business. First, I treat my employees very well. Second, I made sure the family owned a clear majority of all the stock. You were never going to take over my company, even if every other shareholder voted in your favor."

"But Chord . . ."

"Chord's a pompous ass who doesn't do his homework. If he did, then he would have discovered the family owns all those little trusts you thought so little of. Now, Mr. Eldrich, I'm sorry, but I will be relieving you as CEO at the shareholders' meeting next month. Or you can just save yourself the embarrassment and resign. The rest of you are free to hand in your resignations as well, or you're more than welcome to participate in my vetting process. Your choice." Elle let out a happy breath and beamed at the group. "I'll just let that soak in. Good day, gentlemen."

Elle turned on her heel and walked out with Reid following. The room was completely silent as she started down the hall. "I give it three, two, one . . ." Voices erupted and she was pretty sure Mr. Eldrich had just thrown his glass and shattered it against the door.

"Wow, sis. I had no idea you had to deal with this every day. That made me think about the way I treat the women in my employ. I hope I'm not a jerk like that. How do you put up with it?" Reid asked as he pressed the Down button on the elevator.

The doors opened and Elle walked in. "You have to have tough skin. Sometimes you can change their opinions of women executives and sometimes you can't. But if you hold strong, take some risks, and are willing to push for what you believe in, then you'll succeed. You can't just wait for things to be handed to you. You have to make the leap and fight for what you want."

"Dad would be proud of you." Reid shifted the box under one arm and squeezed her shoulder. "I'm very proud of you, too."

"Thanks, Reid. It's good to have you home again."

"It's good to be home. And now that I know you're such a badass, we're going to have a lot of fun."

"Yes, we are."

The elevator opened and Elle felt a deep sense of joy fill her. She'd fought off another takeover. After Mary released her statement, the whole business world would know she was in it for the long run. Plus she had a fiancé who loved and supported her, waiting to hear how it went. Yes, the future was definitely going to be fun.

Chapter Twenty-Six

Three months later . . .

D rake sat next to Elle on her office couch as they went over plans for the resort with Reid. Drake's computer junkies had taken to the project with vigor, and he had the first rough sketches of their plans. Elle placed her hand in his and squeezed. They were getting married in two months and hadn't planned a thing. Their mothers and Shirley had taken over. Instead of fighting it, Drake and Elle just went along with whatever they planned. Neither of them cared if the wedding colors were navy, yellow, or hot pink. They just cared about living happily ever after.

"Oh, I forgot. We closed on the house this morning and will be moving in over the weekend. We took the last load out of Elle's condo last night. Here are the keys to Elle's place, well . . . your place now." Drake took the keys out of his pocket and tossed them to Reid.

"Thanks. I know I could have stayed at a hotel for these past two weeks, but Mom was so excited to have me at home. It'll be good to move into my own space." Reid snagged the keys out of the air and put them in his pocket.

"Your mother loved having you. You're a good son."

Drake, Elle, and Reid looked around and saw no one.

Soon they heard the sharp piercing squeal of a hearing aid and then the walker appeared at the office door.

"Wanted for felony sexiness," Reid read off the bumper sticker on the front of Shirley's walker.

"Like it? Damien gave it to me. Such a nice man."

"Who's Damien? Do you have a boyfriend?" Reid asked, amazed.

"Oh no. I've done enough laundry for men in my life. Nope, I'm a use-'em-and-leave-'em type." Drake choked on his drink and Reid's eyes grew as large as saucers while Elle snickered. "Nope, Damien is Mallory's beau. He's a grade A specimen, but what else would you expect from the Secret Service?"

Reid snorted. "Mallory is dating a Secret Service agent? Yeah, right. He must be a trust fund brat looking for something to amuse him."

Elle jumped to her best friend's defense. "He's no such thing. And Mallory wouldn't date someone like that. Besides, you're a trust fund brat. What happened between you two? Why don't you like her?"

"Nothing. Back to these plans. The airstrip has been started and looks good. My pilot, Troy, is overseeing it and working with the builders to make sure we have everything we need. I also looked into the arena. I don't think it will work with so many sporting venues available in the area, but I do think we can do a concert hall. It will be big enough to draw top names for 'intimate' performances. We could also do boxing and a few other smaller events."

Elle shook her head at his change of subject but went with it. Whatever happened between them was bad enough to last fifteen years and was still between them. No more asking, Elle swore to herself. "That sounds good. Then we won't have to worry about selling it out constantly."

"Exactly. I've also built a dock, a white gazebo, and bought some boats for the lake. It will make a beautiful spot for weddings. The only thing still needed in that area is a lakefront restaurant and banquet hall."

"I really like that plan. Good job, Reid."

"Thanks." Reid looked at Drake and put on his overly excited smile. "Wanna help me move in? I'll pay you in beer."

Drake laughed. "Sounds good."

He'd never had a brother before. But over the past couple of months, he and Reid had grown close. There was a serious side to him that his sisters didn't want to, or simply couldn't, see. They thought he was such a playboy. But he spent many nights hanging out with Drake, talking business or sports without a woman in sight.

Drake leaned over and kissed Elle on the lips. It was the best thing about being with her — those simple kisses. The emotion they could convey was amazing. They could have whole conversations without saying a word. This kiss told him she'd be waiting for him tonight with nothing on. He wondered how fast he could move all of Reid's things.

"I love you."

"Love you, too." Elle smiled and he knew for certain he could be home by six, even if it meant carrying every box himself.

Elle watched her brother and her future husband head out of the office, talking and laughing. Shirley scooted over and took the seat Reid just left.

"You knocked up yet?"

"Shirley!"

"What, it's an easy question."

Elle rolled her eyes. "Did my mother bribe you with an

apple pie to ask me that?"

Shirley didn't bother blushing at being caught. "You'd be crazy to turn down one of her pies. So, what do I tell her?"

"No, I'm not knocked up. Can we at least get married and enjoy being newlyweds first?"

"Have you met your mother?"

Elle let out a long-suffering breath. Oh God, she was turning into the old Mary. As if on cue, Mary walked into the office with Allegra, Bree, Finn, and Jessica. Mary had blossomed over the past few months. She was more confident, dressed beautifully, and even managed to cut out the hourly phone calls with her mother.

"Mary, another beautiful dress." Elle smiled up at her cousin who blushed at the compliment.

"Thank you. It was a gift."

"A gift? From whom, because I need to hire them," Allegra teased.

"Humph. Where have you all been?" Shirley asked. "It's from her boyfriend."

"Boyfriend?" they all asked together as Mary's face turned a deeper shade of red.

"Who are you dating?" Bree asked.

"How long have you been dating?" Allegra added.

"Do you all know nothing?" Shirley shook her head. "She's been dating Drake's assistant, Phillip, for a little over three months."

"What?" Elle was shocked. Drake had said nothing about it, which meant he probably didn't know either.

"We've been keeping it quiet. I didn't want my mother interfering."

"Good call, dear," Shirley clucked. "He's a hottie."

"Wait, four months." Elle thought back to the Secret

Service's accusations of Mary. "Did you go out with him sometimes for lunch when you first started dating?"

"Yes. It's how we met. He asked me out for lunch after the press conference."

Elle looked around the room and saw disbelief, but happiness on everyone's faces as she laughed privately. No wonder Mary didn't say anything. No one would have believed her back then. It just went to show how much she had matured.

"Wait, what about Dean?" Allegra asked.

Mary wrinkled her nose as if she smelled something bad. "He's such a player. I just didn't realize it until I met a real man. Now I understand what you guys have been telling me all these years."

Elle couldn't wait to tell her mother. But first she needed to get some work done. Getting back to the reason she called them all to the office, Elle smiled at the full room. "Well, this meeting started off with good news. I hope to expand on it. Finn, I've looked over your proposal. I'm following your advice, and with some of the extra money we made on the sale of the Titan-owned newspapers, I'm going to put it toward an entertainment and sports agency."

A smile broke out across Finn's face as he looked to Allegra first. She smiled back before he came to shake Elle's hand. Allegra had helped show Finn the ropes. She had taught him how to look into a company's financials, assets, debts, and potential. It was hard, but Elle was going to have to admit her baby sister was a force all of her own in the business world.

"Thank you so much. I won't let you down."

"I know you won't. And we're all here to help. Now, go move into your new office. Shirley, can you do the honors of showing it to him?"

"Of course. Come on, young man." Finn couldn't stop smiling as he held out his arm for Shirley to take. They walked out of the room with Shirley telling him everything people try to get away with in their offices.

"Is nothing private?" Elle asked her cousin and sisters.

"No!" came Shirley's reply from down the hall, and the girls broke out into laughter.

"Mary, can you write up a press release announcing Simpson Entertainment Agency and introducing Finn as the new vice president of operations. Double-check with him, but I think he already has some clients lined up in addition to the list I gave you."

"Sure thing." Mary jumped with excitement and headed off to do her job.

"I can't believe that's our cousin," Allegra whispered as she watched Mary stride out of the office.

"Good for her." Bree grinned.

Elle looked to her secretary. "Jessica, I'm sorry, but you're no longer going to be my secretary."

Jessica's face fell. "You're firing me?"

"Goodness no. I'm promoting you to Director of Finance. I want you to oversee the financial branch and report directly to me. I'm going to focus on managing our growing company even more. We have so many adventures on the horizon and I can't wait to enjoy them."

"Director of Finance . . . I can't believe it. Thank you so much."

"You deserve it. Go on, pack up your desk, and move into the empty office next to mine."

"Yes, ma'am." Jessica hurried from the room and Elle knew she had made the right choice. Jessica had learned by her side for the past eight years. No one knew more about Elle's job and what it entailed than Jessica.

Bree waited until the door shut before speaking. "I'm glad it's just us now. I'm having some issues with the corporate center I'm working on."

"Did the steel make it on time?" Elle asked as she reached for the project folder.

"Yes. And we were able to finish the foundation and the first ten floors. But the architect has this fancy dome of glass and steel that he wants to put in, but he keeps adjusting it. So we're stuck until he finalizes his plans. It's costing us money to keep Simpson Construction on site. I'm moving the guys to other projects, but that's only going to cover us for a little while."

"That is a problem. Has the architect been on the site to evaluate?" Elle wondered as she flipped through her notes looking for his name.

"No. He's from London. I've left message after message for him, but he hasn't gotten back to me yet."

"Who is he and why does he think he's so special he can keep everyone waiting?" Allegra asked. "And trust me, I work with divas. They at least get the job done. They know that I'll take my business elsewhere if they don't."

"That's part of the problem. This center isn't fully owned by us. We're the contractors and minority owner. We provide the steel and the construction. Two other companies actually own the majority of the building. They're the ones who hired Logan Ward, not me," Bree explained.

"I take it you've been playing nice so far?" Elle knew her sister. She always tried sugar first, but when she was pushed, she was anything but nice.

"Yes."

"Then I think it's time for you to stop being nice. Get the job done, Bree."

"Oh, bitchy Bree gets to make an appearance. Poor guy." Allegra laughed and Bree just looked annoyed. Elle knew her sister had to be tough with the guys on site when necessary, but she always hated it. When she had to stand her ground, it usually involved tears, and not Bree's.

"I'll go call him now. If I have to, I'll have Troy fly me to London so I can grab him by the willy and drag him over here to make a decision." Bree stood up and stalked from the room.

"You go, girl," Allegra called after her.

"Is everything going all right with you, Allegra?" Elle had been wondering that. While she was her perky self, she did sometimes catch Allegra looking at her phone with a frown.

"It's peachy. But, I'd better get to work. I'm looking over the final designs for Bellerose's fall line."

"Okay, but know I'm here if you need anything."

"I know." Allegra bent down and hugged her. "You're the best big sis."

"You're a pretty awesome little sis. See you at the housewarming on Sunday?"

"Of course. Someone is going to have to bring a little style into your home." Allegra gave a wink and headed to her office.

Elle sat back and looked around. The last three months had changed her. Her family had stepped up, Simpson Global was growing, and Drake met her at home every night. She couldn't imagine her life getting any better.

Bree stalked to her office. Stupid man, couldn't make a decision. She was going to finish this nightmare of a job if it killed her. Normally she only had to visit the major sites once a month, but this one was such a pain it was starting to take over her life. She suddenly felt like a site manager instead of vice president.

"Get me Mr. Ward on the phone, please. If you can't reach him, then let me talk to his assistant," Bree told her assistant, Noah, as she walked past his desk.

"I'll try. Here's the mail for you."

Bree thanked him and took it into the office. All the mail was open except one letter. She looked at the envelope and felt her body go still. It was marked "personal," which prevented Noah from opening it. But she knew what it was before she even opened it.

With shaky hands, she slid the letter opener along the top and pulled out the green sheet of paper.

Elle walked into Drake's mostly packed house later that evening to find the lights off and a path of candles leading upstairs. She followed them down the hall and into the master bath where a bubble bath sprinkled with rose petals waited for her. Drake stood with a sponge in one hand and a glass of wine in the other.

"Time for your bath, sweetheart."

Elle looked around the room with amazement. It was the most romantic thing she'd ever seen. Not a single light was on. Instead, the counter was filled with candles that danced in the mirror and cast a warm glow around the room.

She grew hot with excitement as Drake stood smiling at her. He didn't rush her, but she knew what he planned to do in the tub. She unbuttoned her suit coat and placed it on the nearby dressing table. Slowly she unbuttoned her silk blouse and shimmied out of her skirt. Having already kicked off her heels in the kitchen, Elle placed one leg on the edge of the tub and slowly rolled the thigh-high silk stocking down her leg.

Drake drank in the sight of her as Elle dropped her bra and panties to the floor and stepped into the tub. Life was just about to get a lot better than she could ever have imagined.

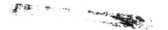

Made in the USA
Lexington, KY
27 May 2015